THIS BOOK BELONGS TO:

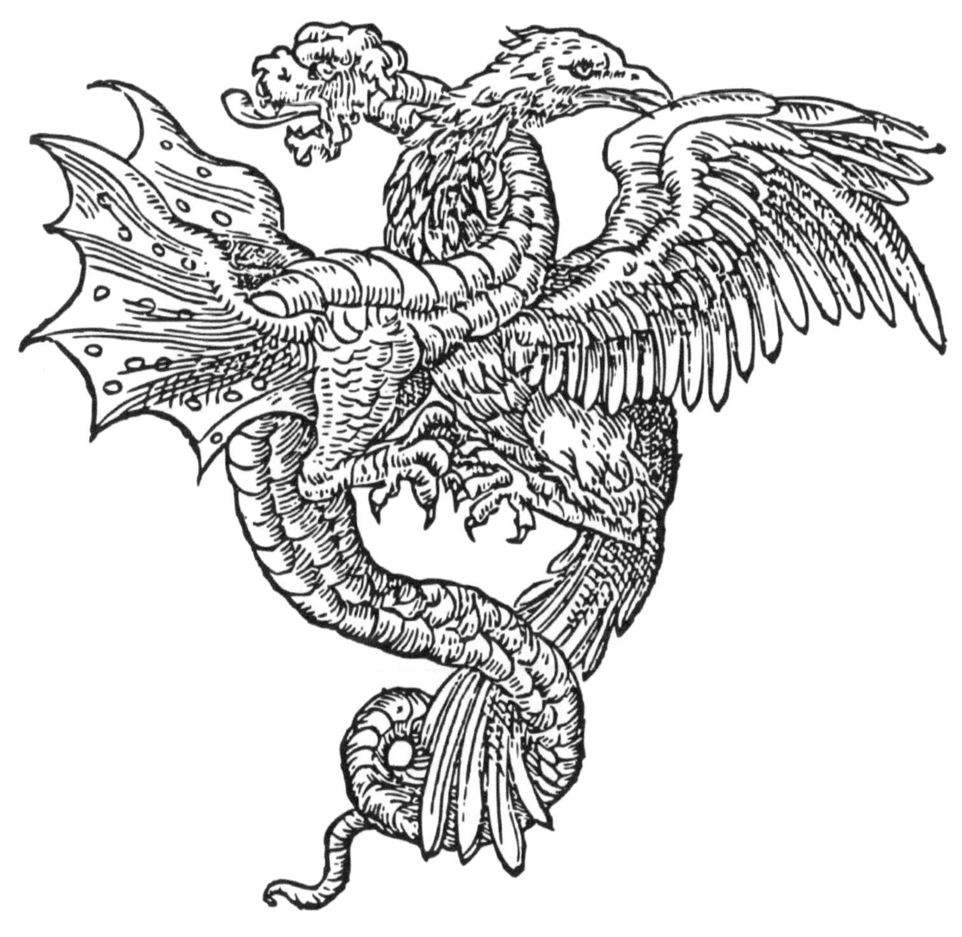

BONUS

Get your Free 50 Coloring Pages

On the Last Page!!

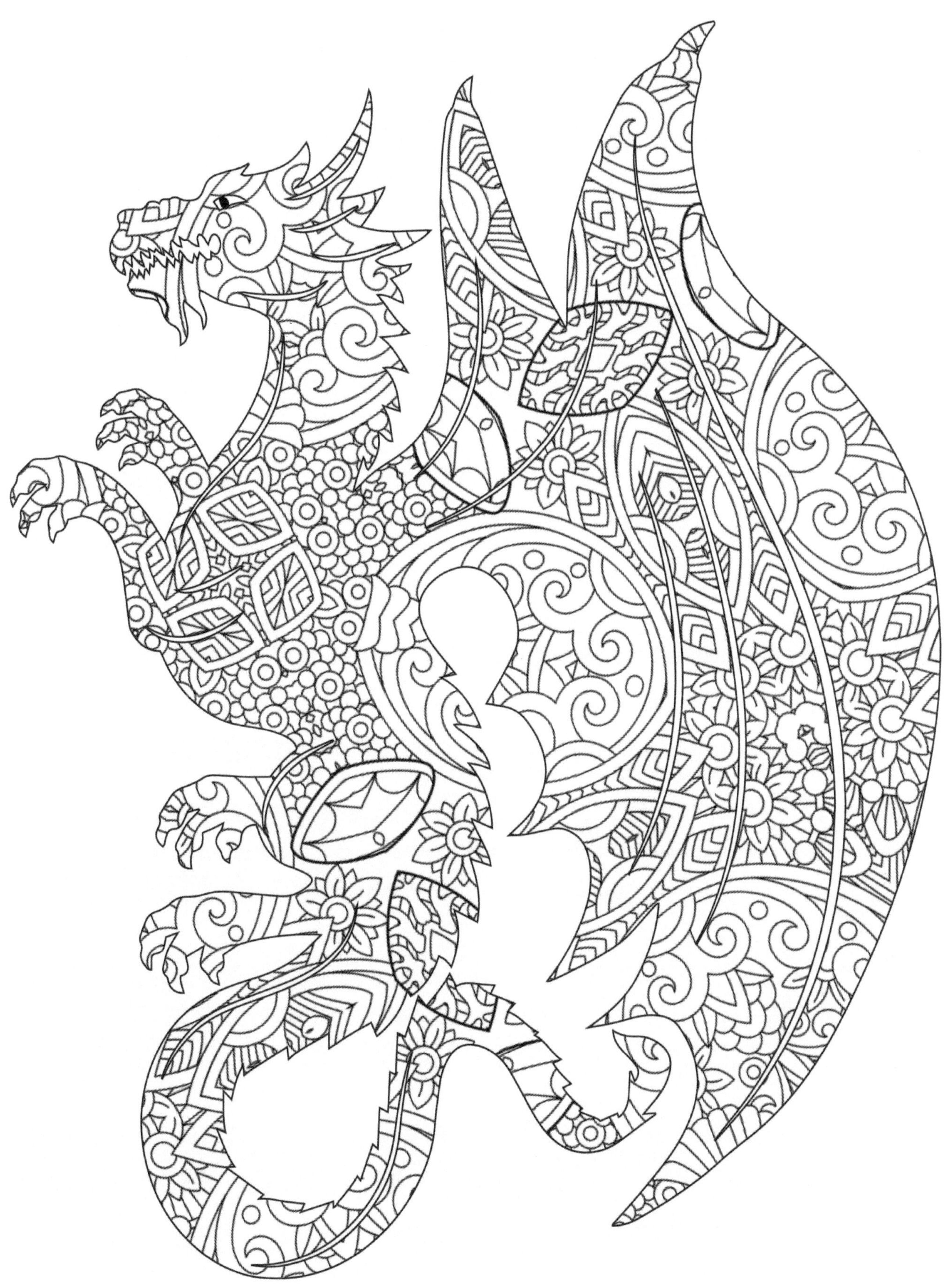

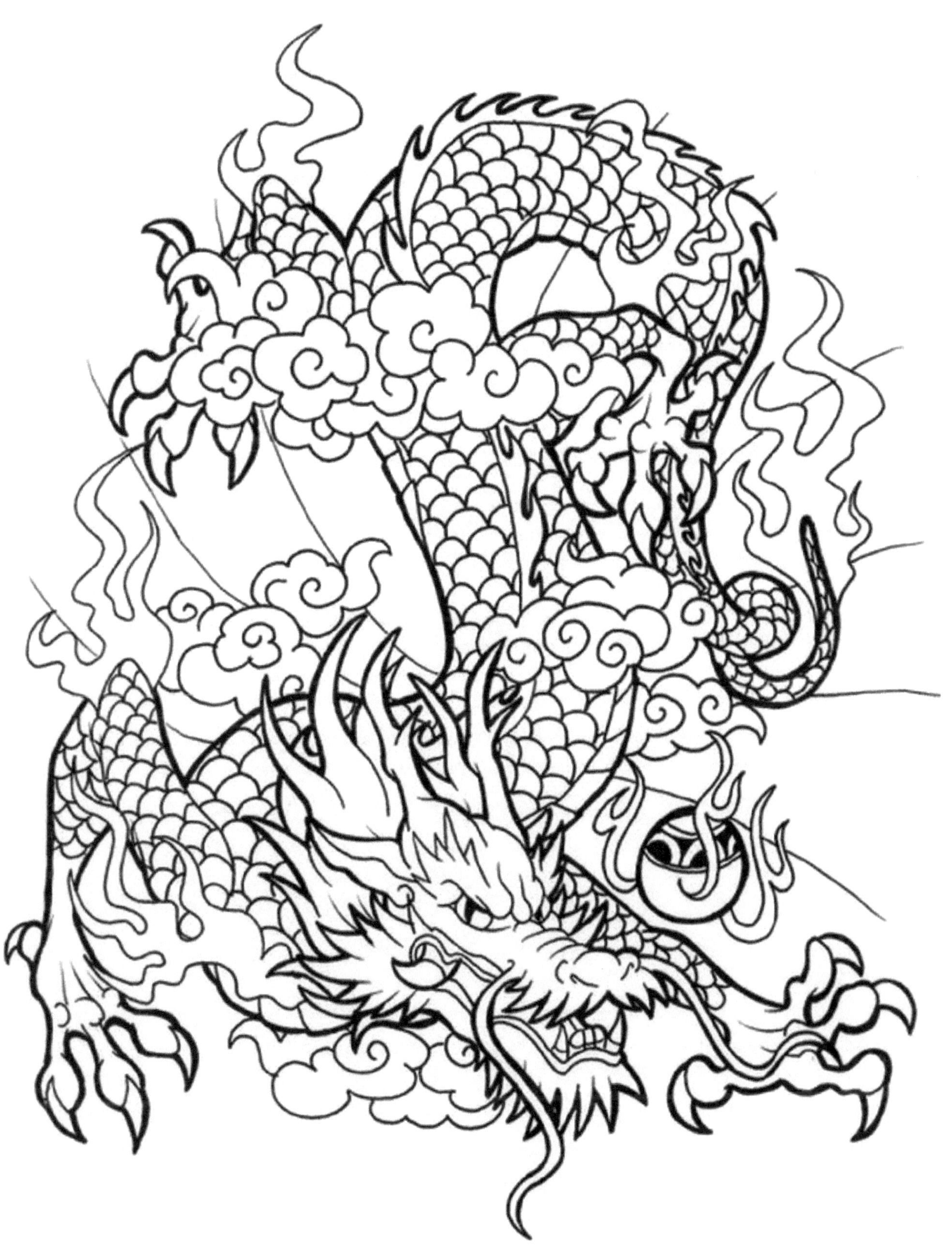

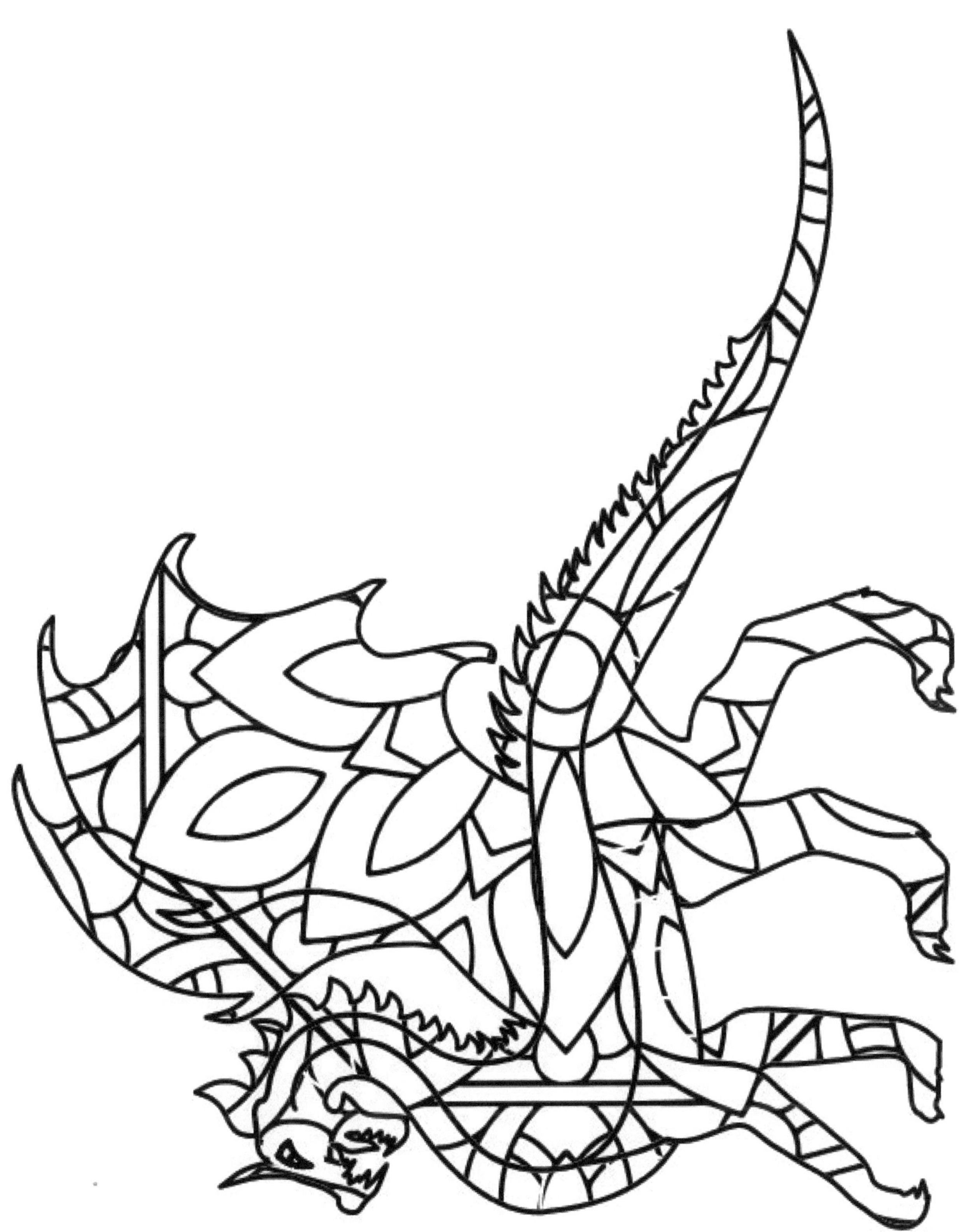

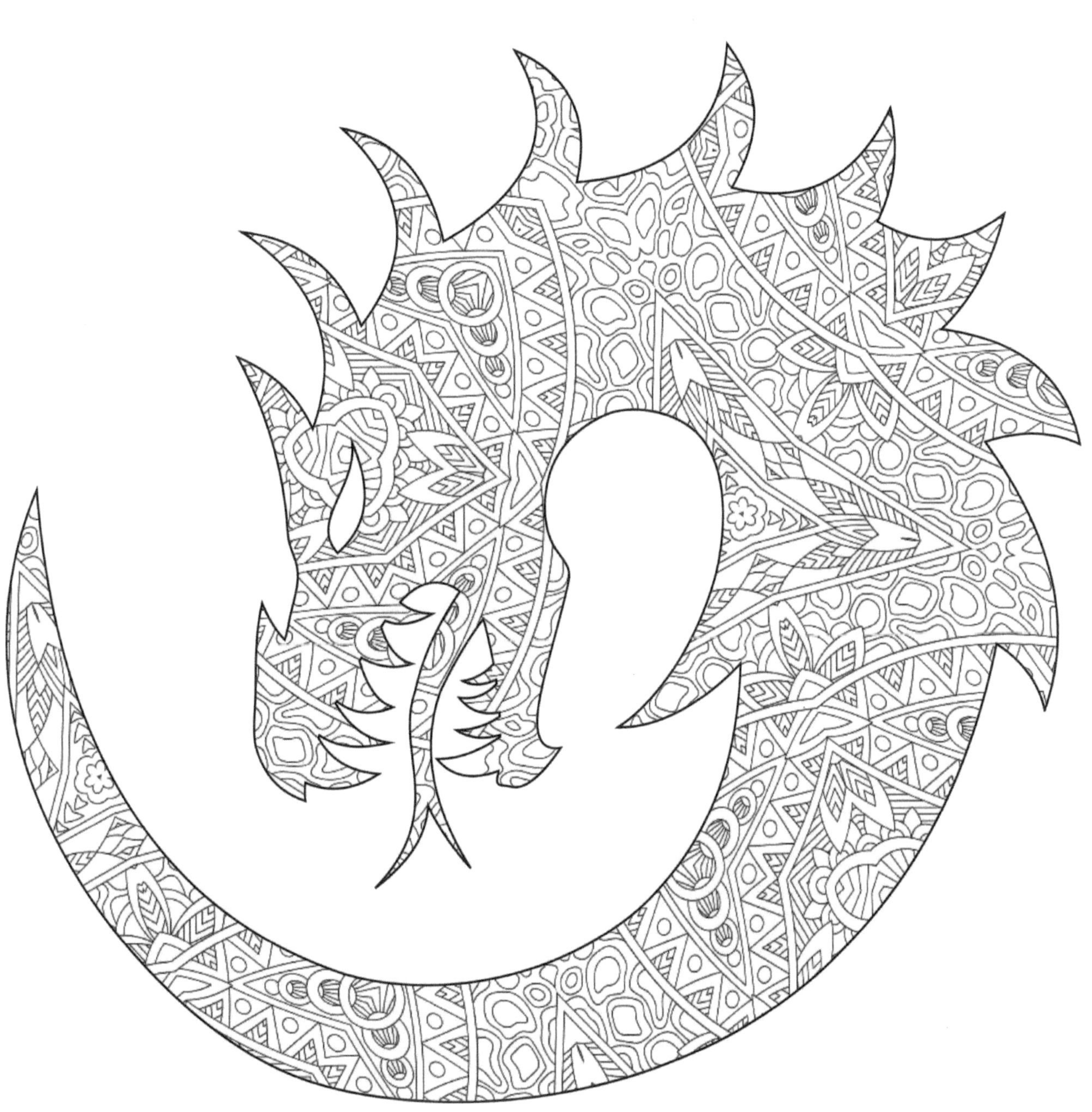

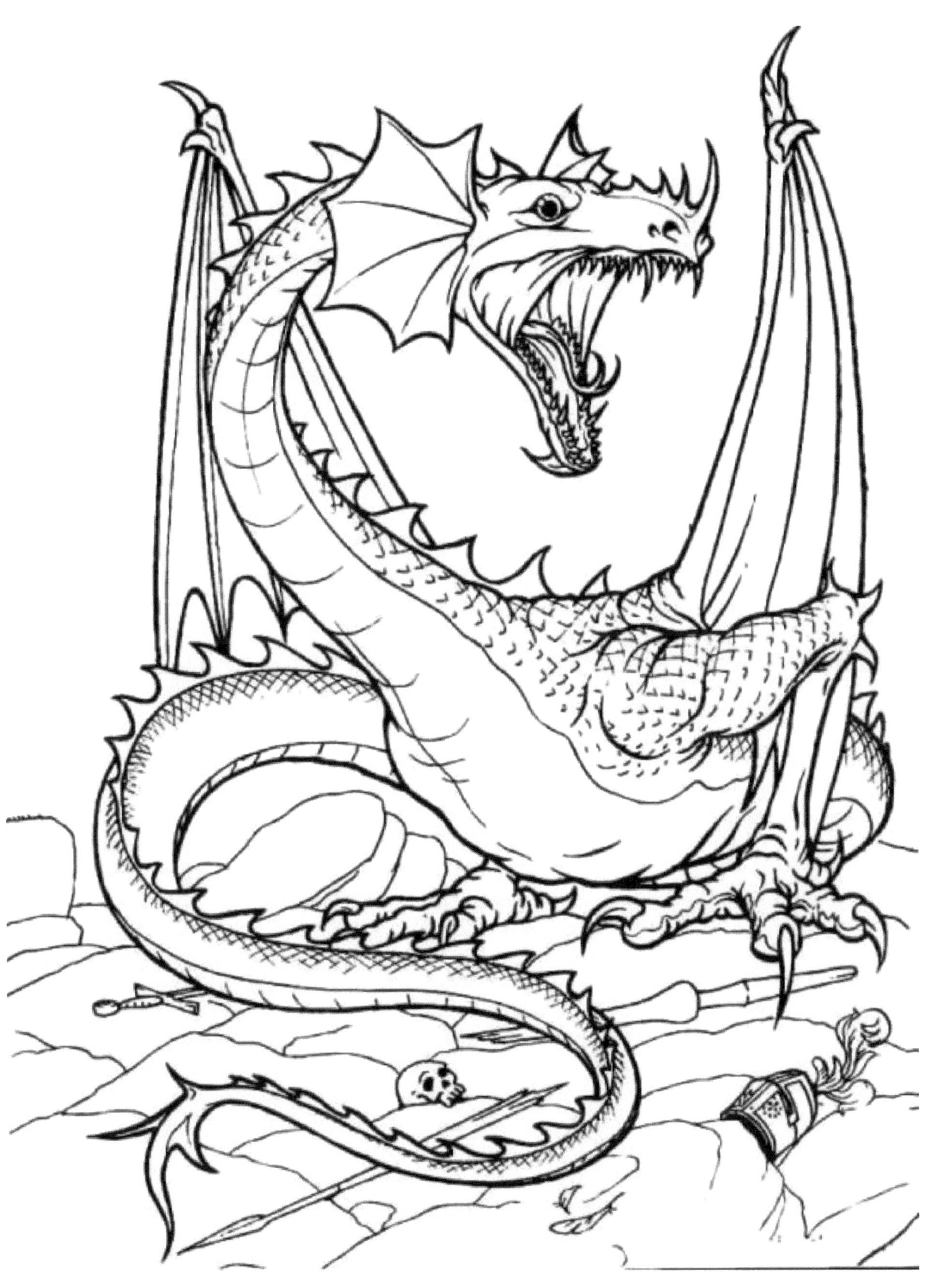

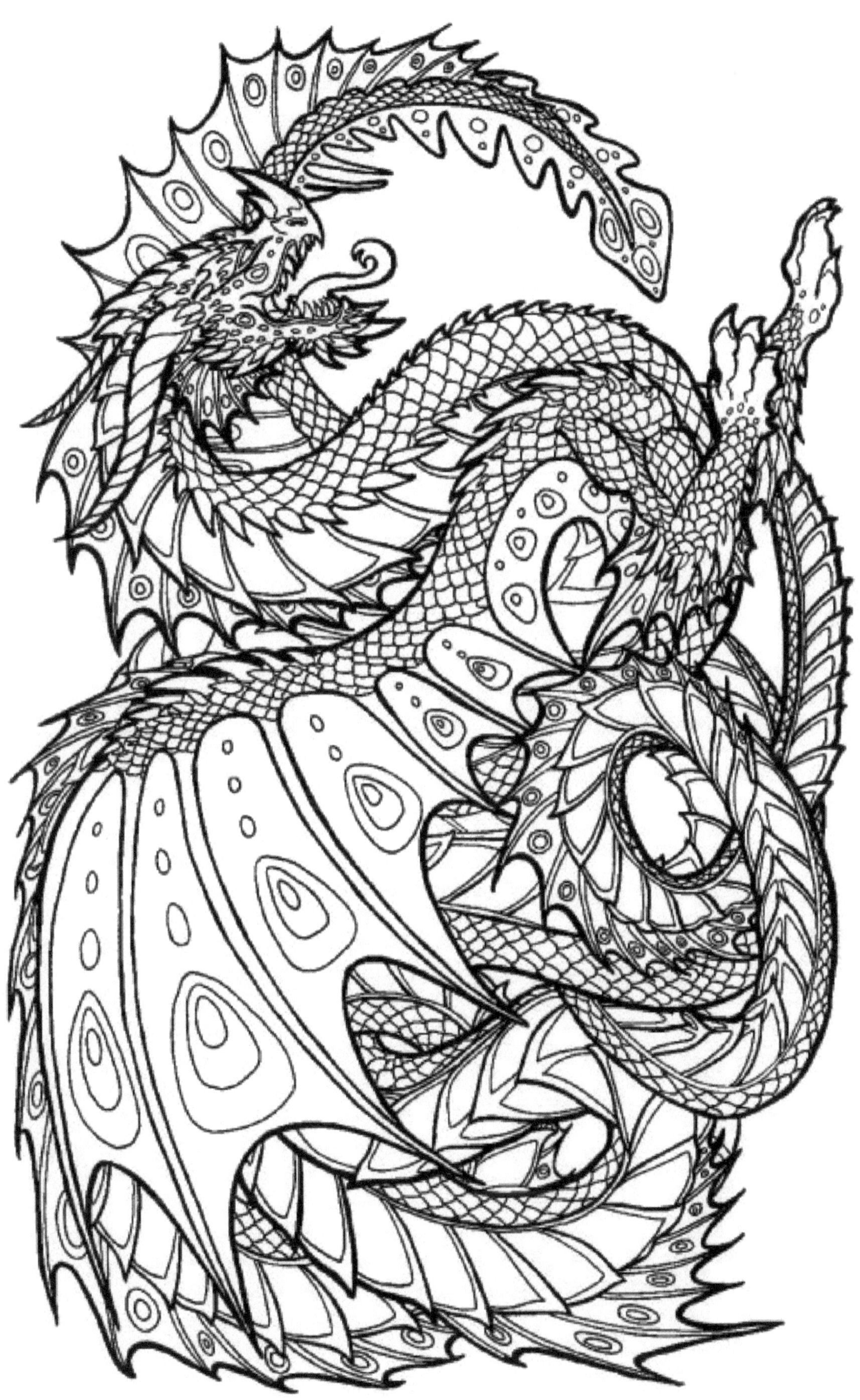

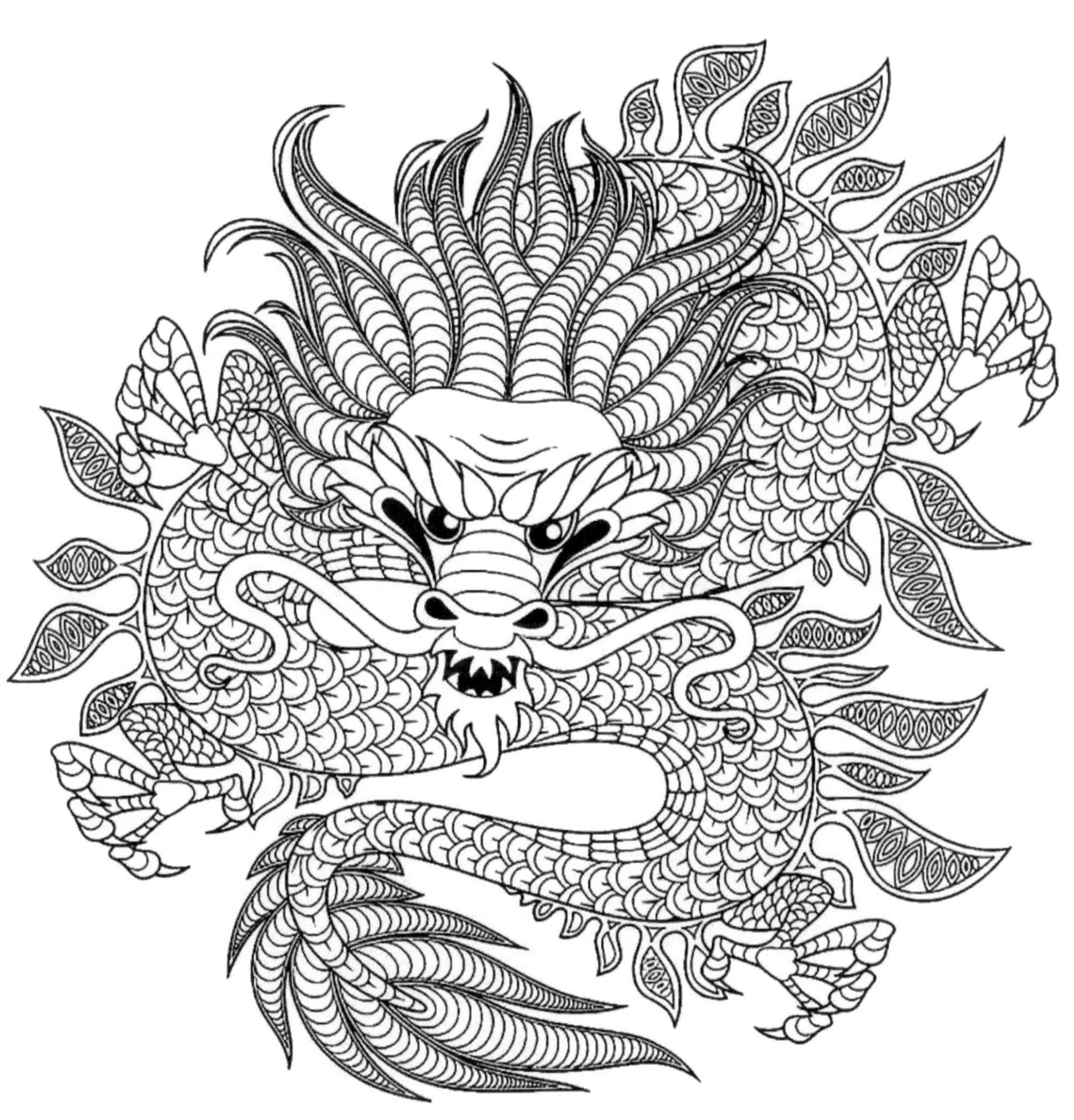

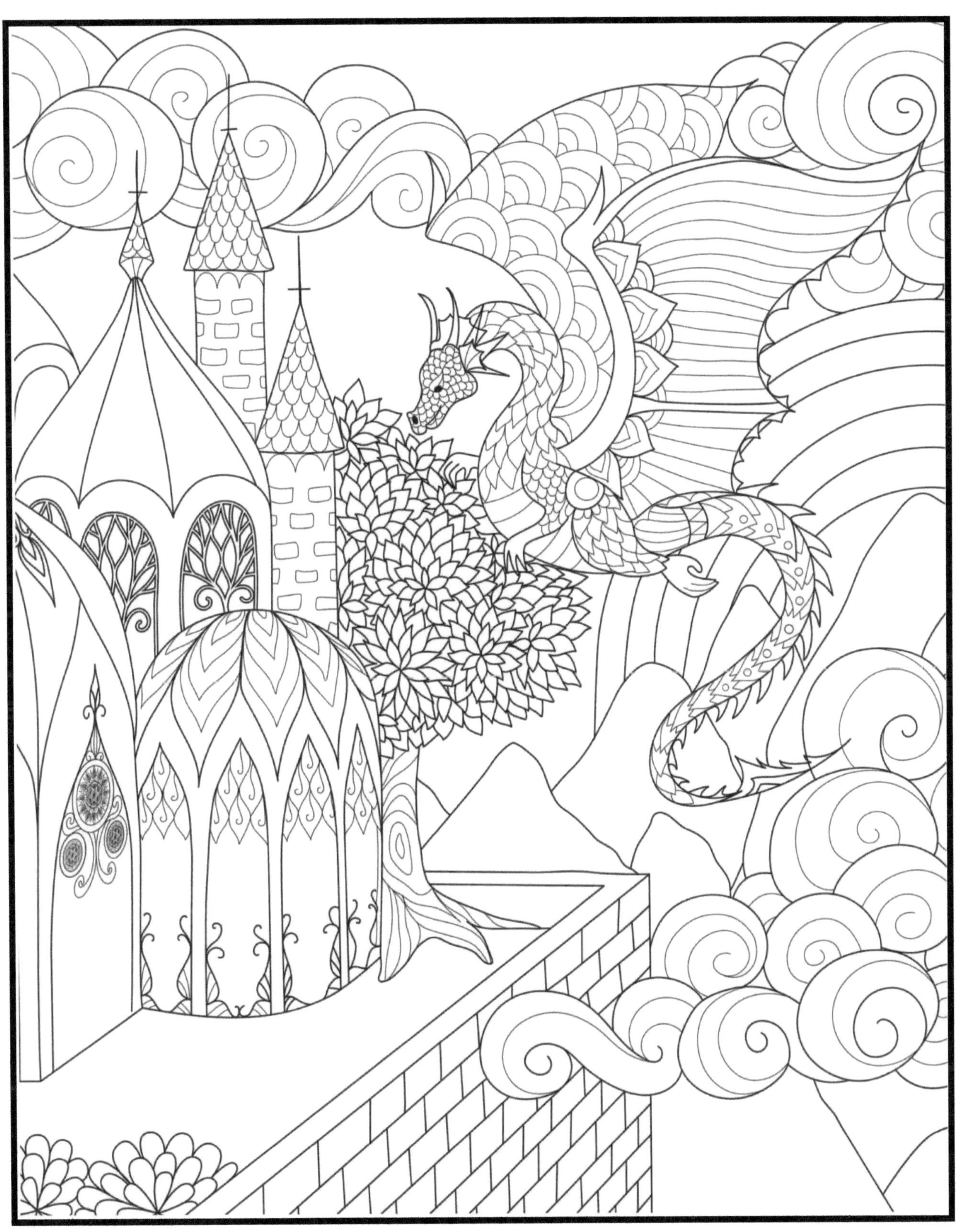

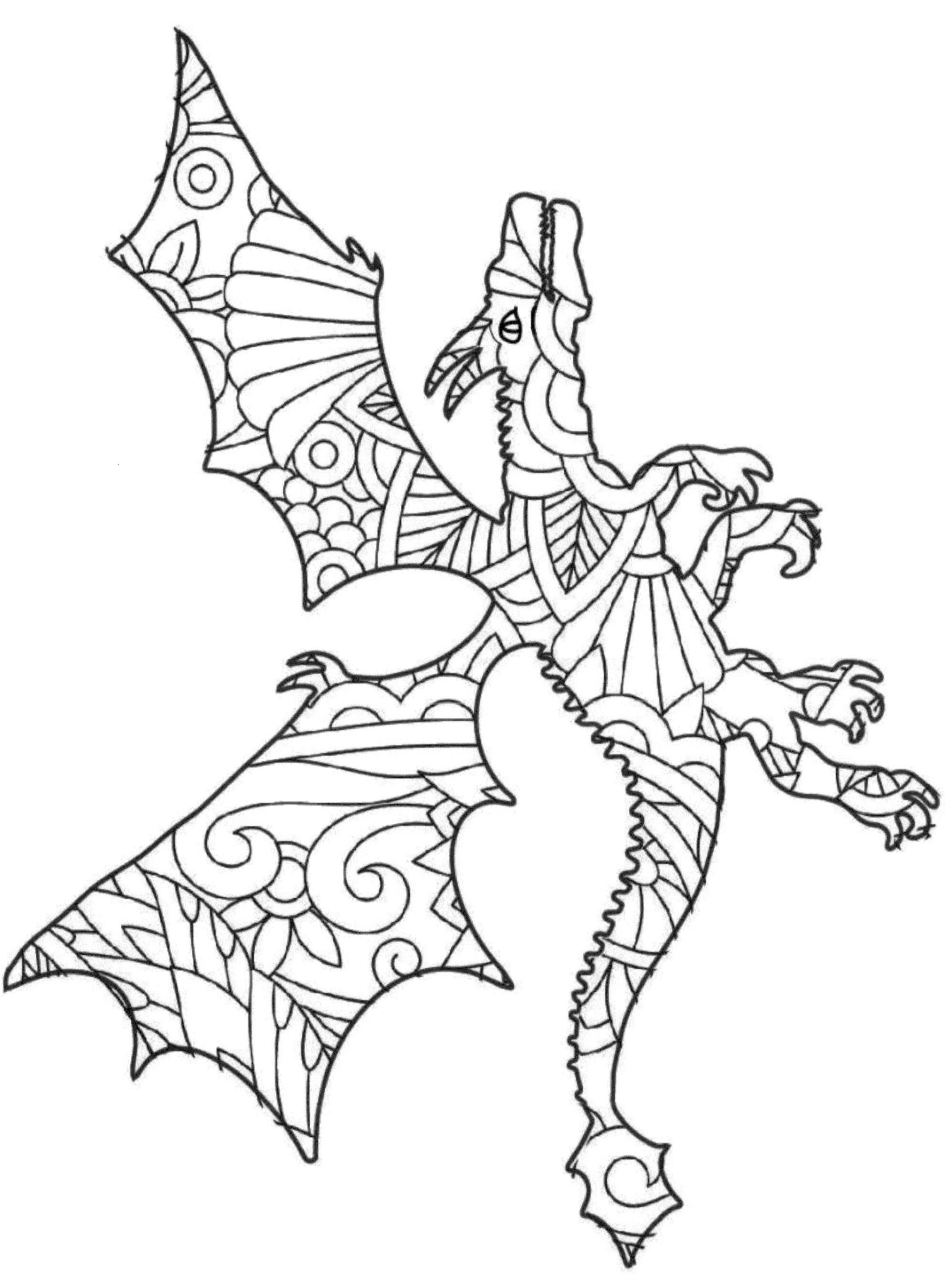

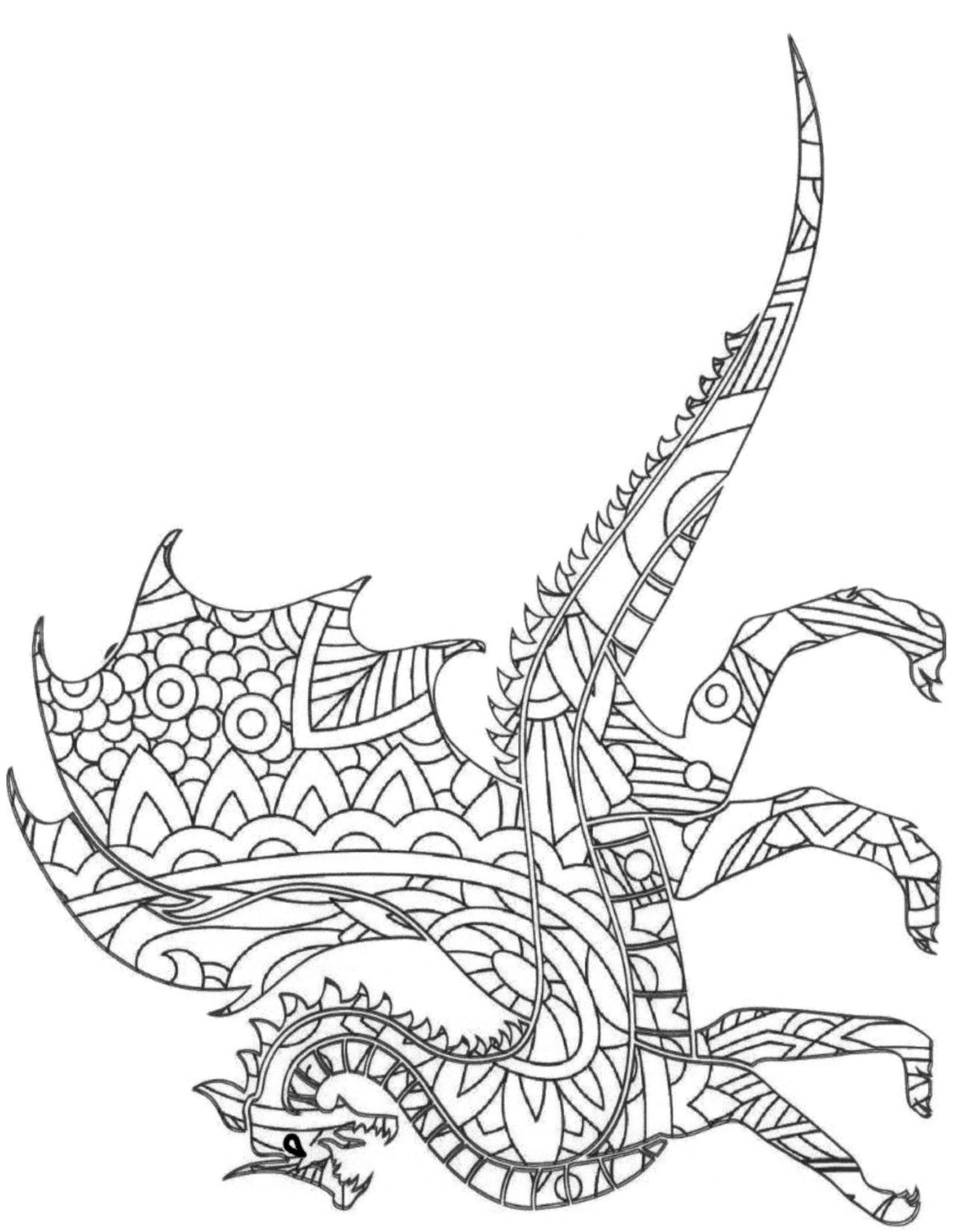

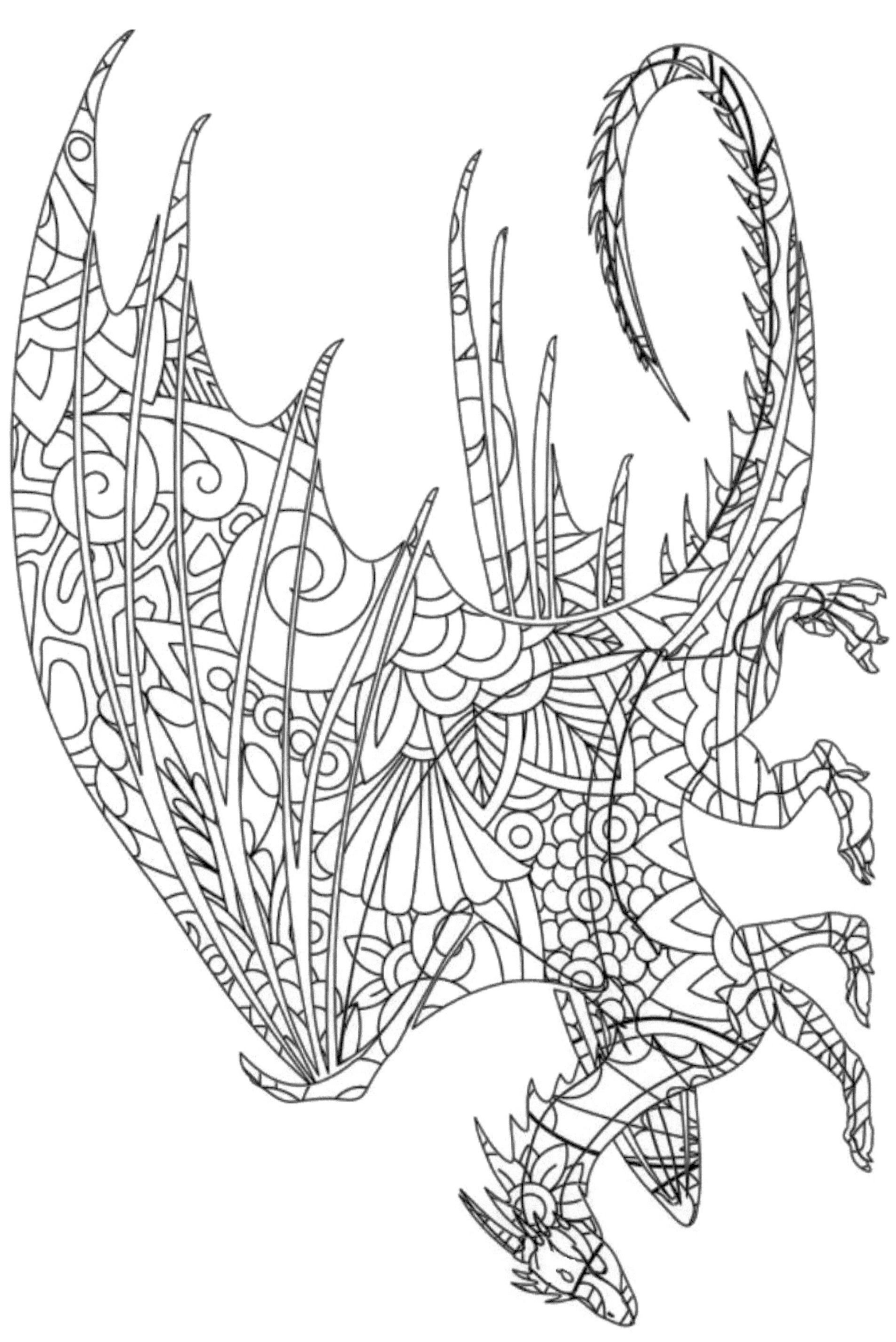

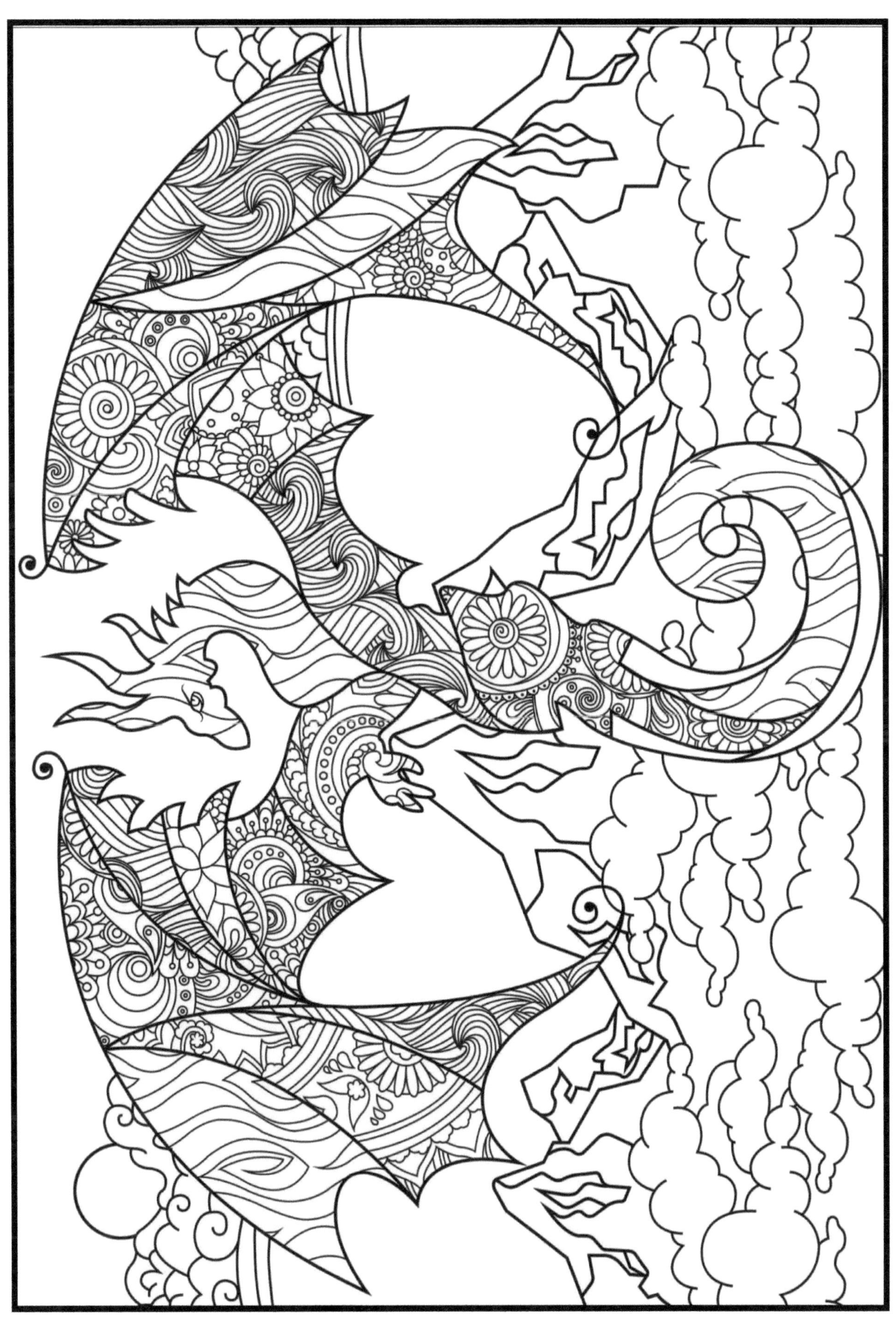

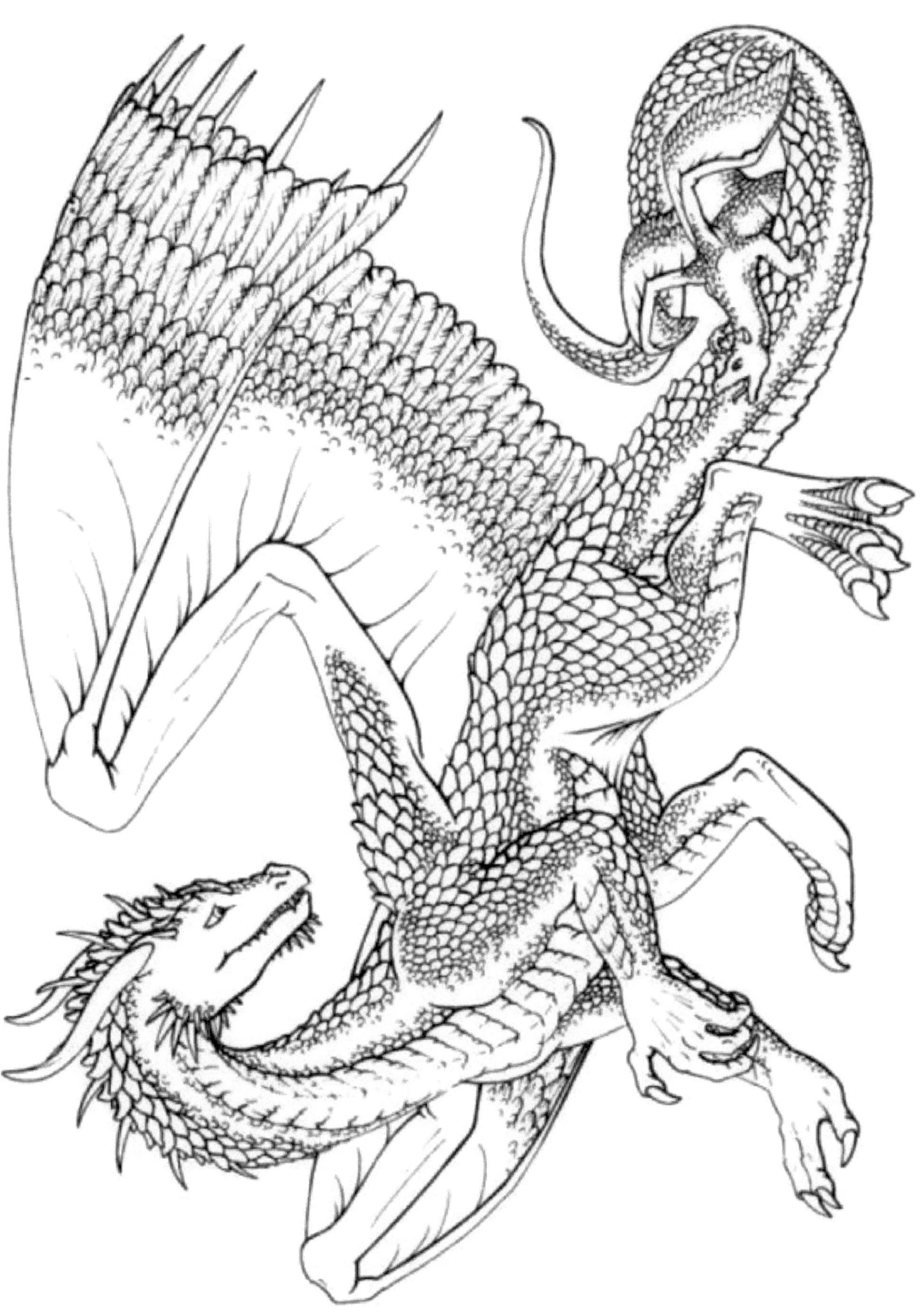

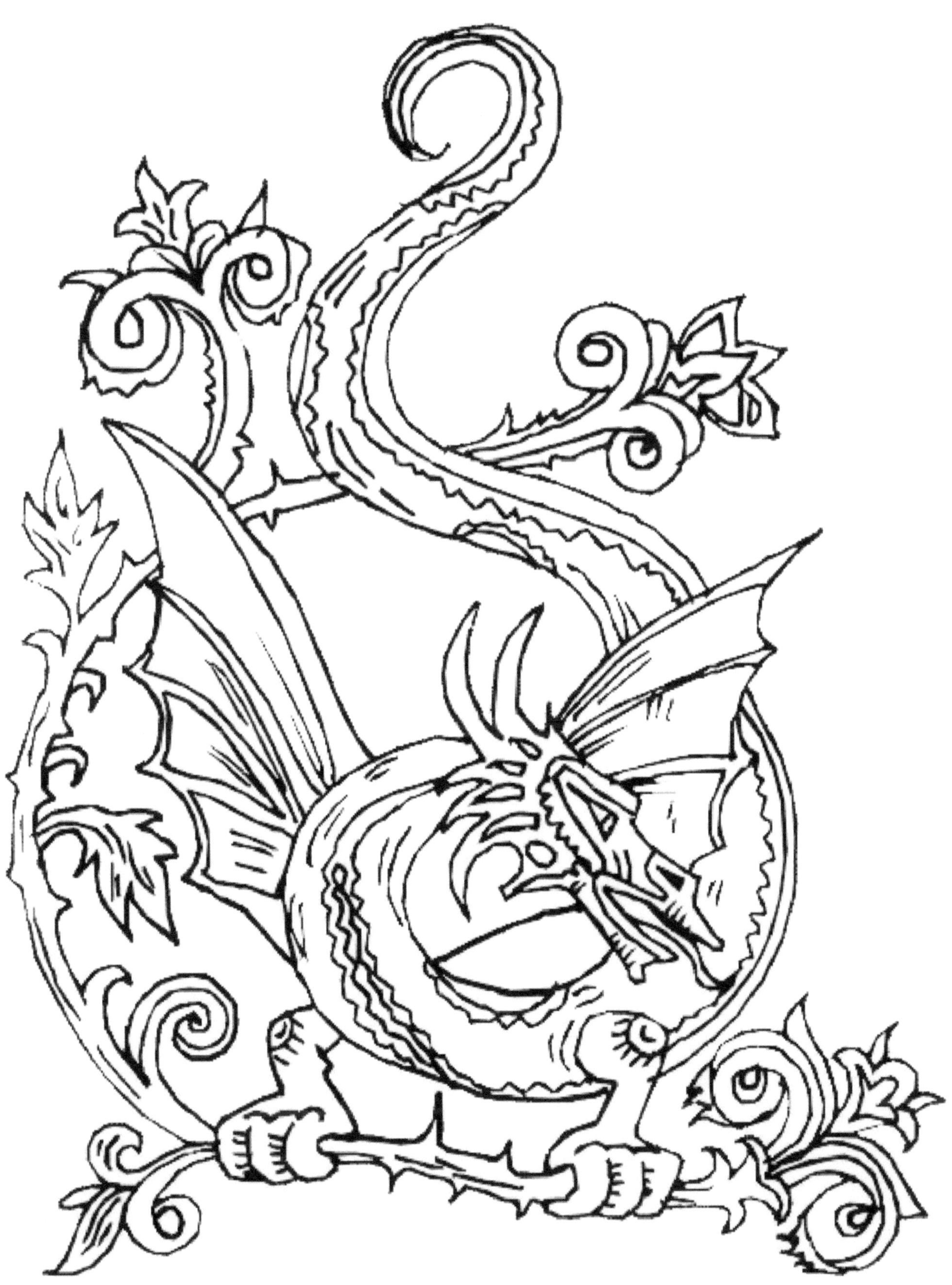

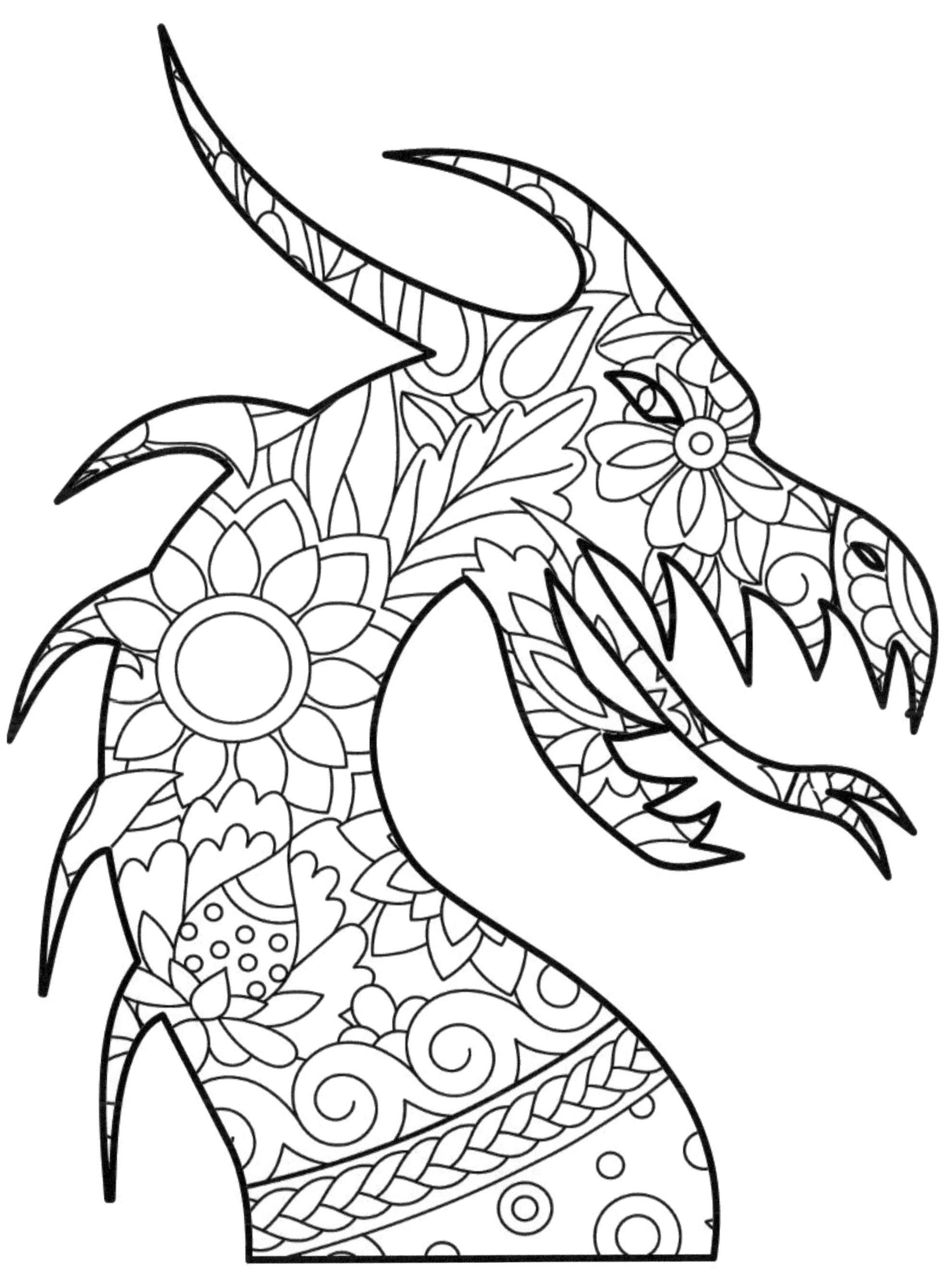

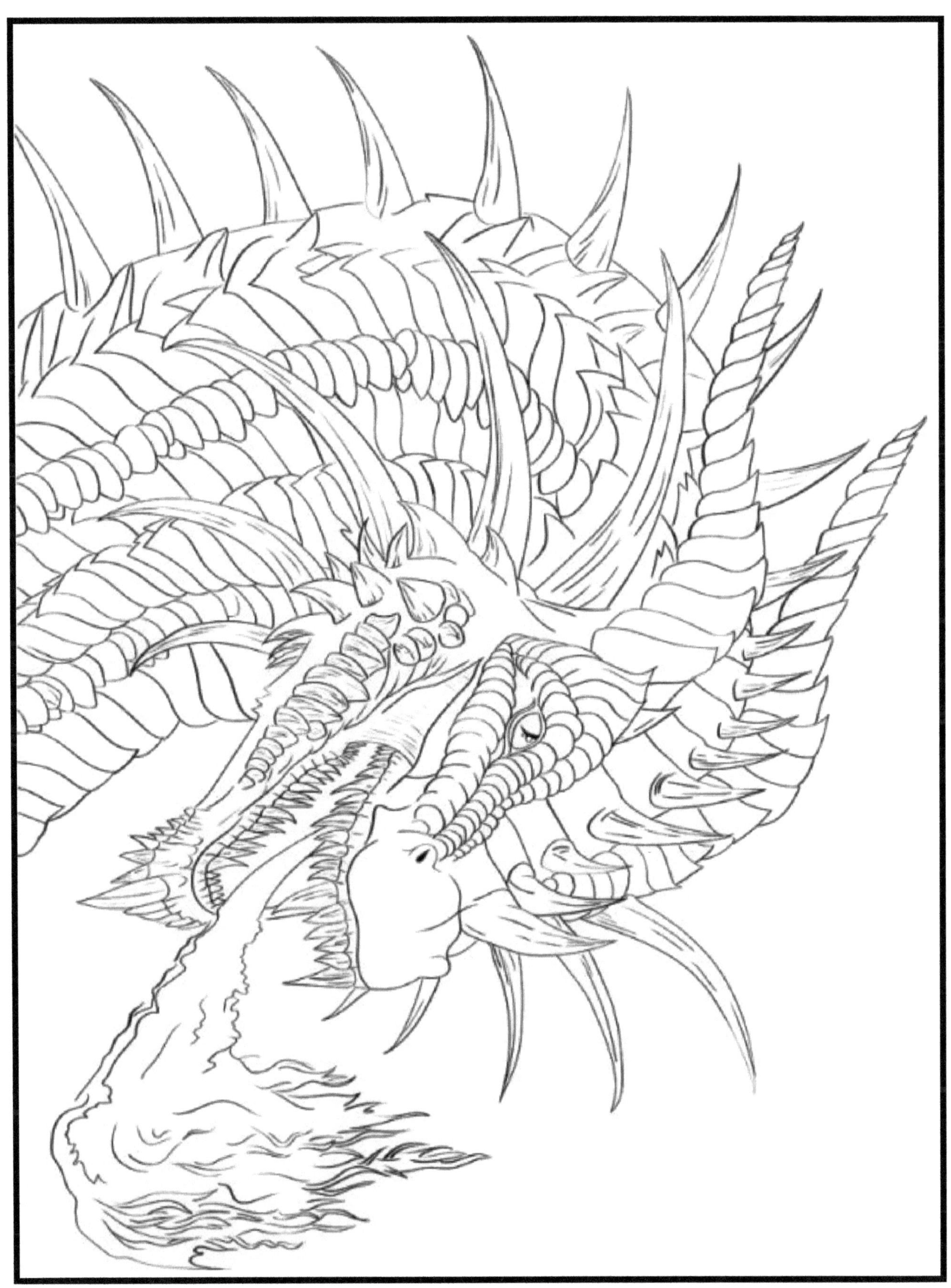

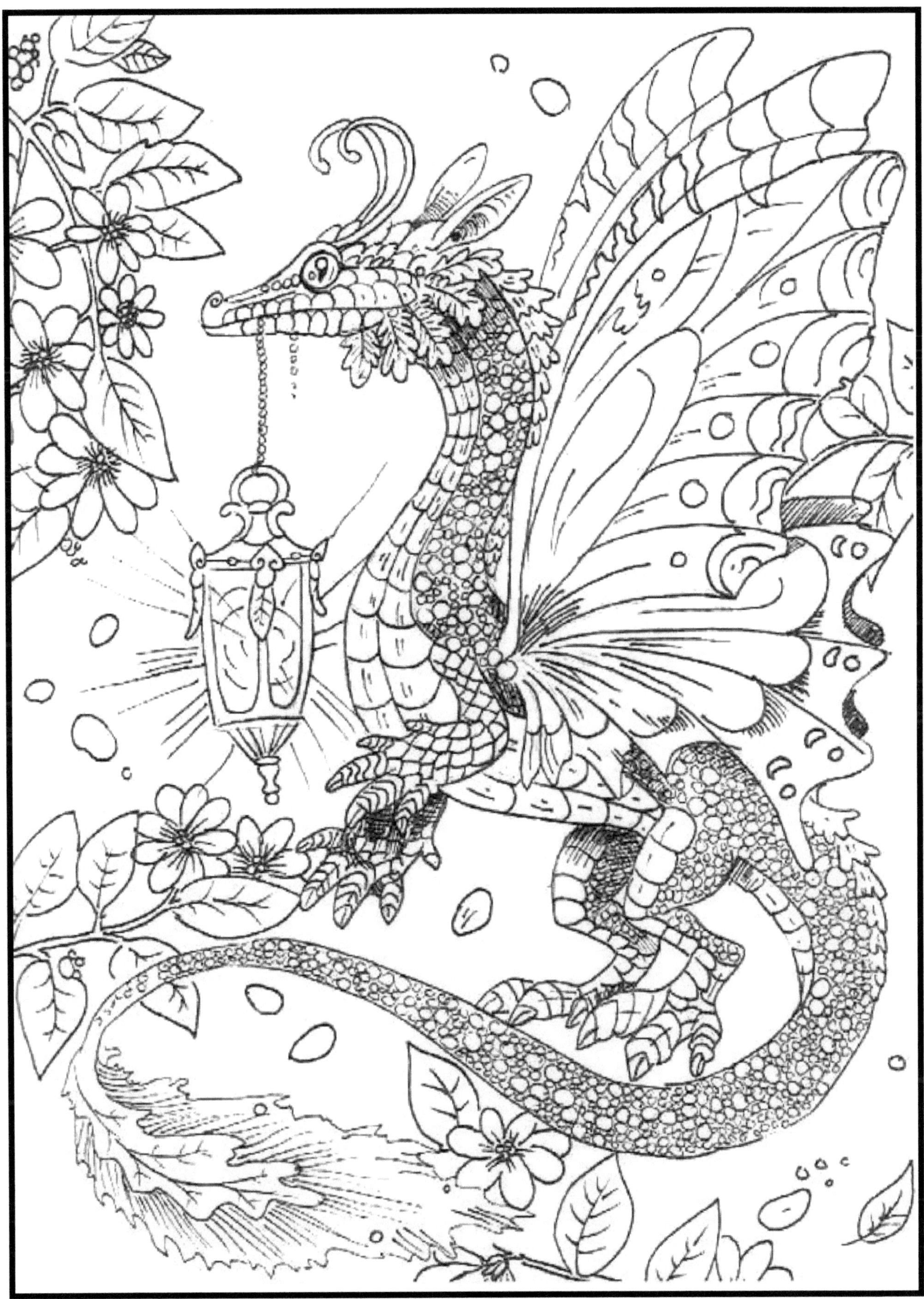

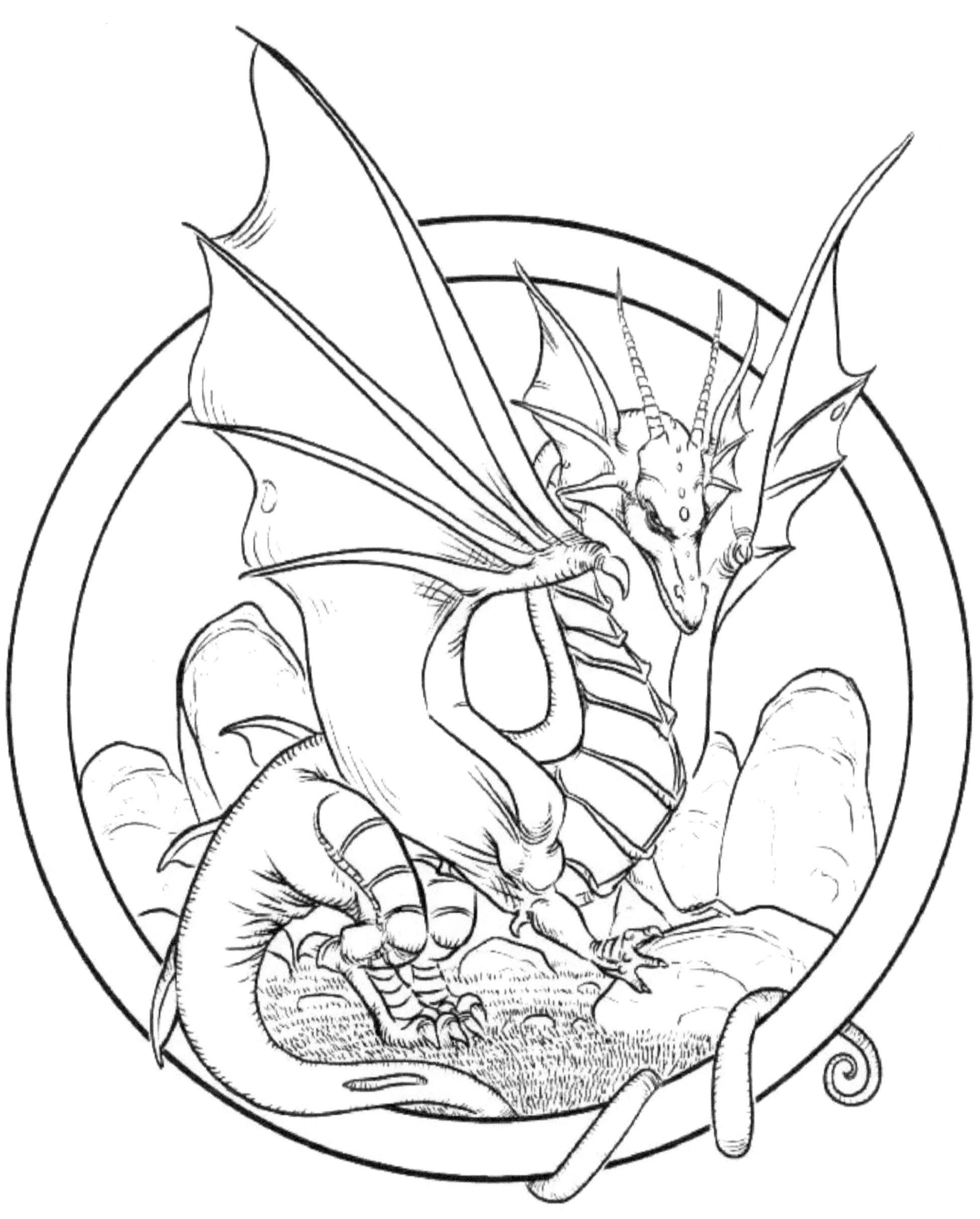

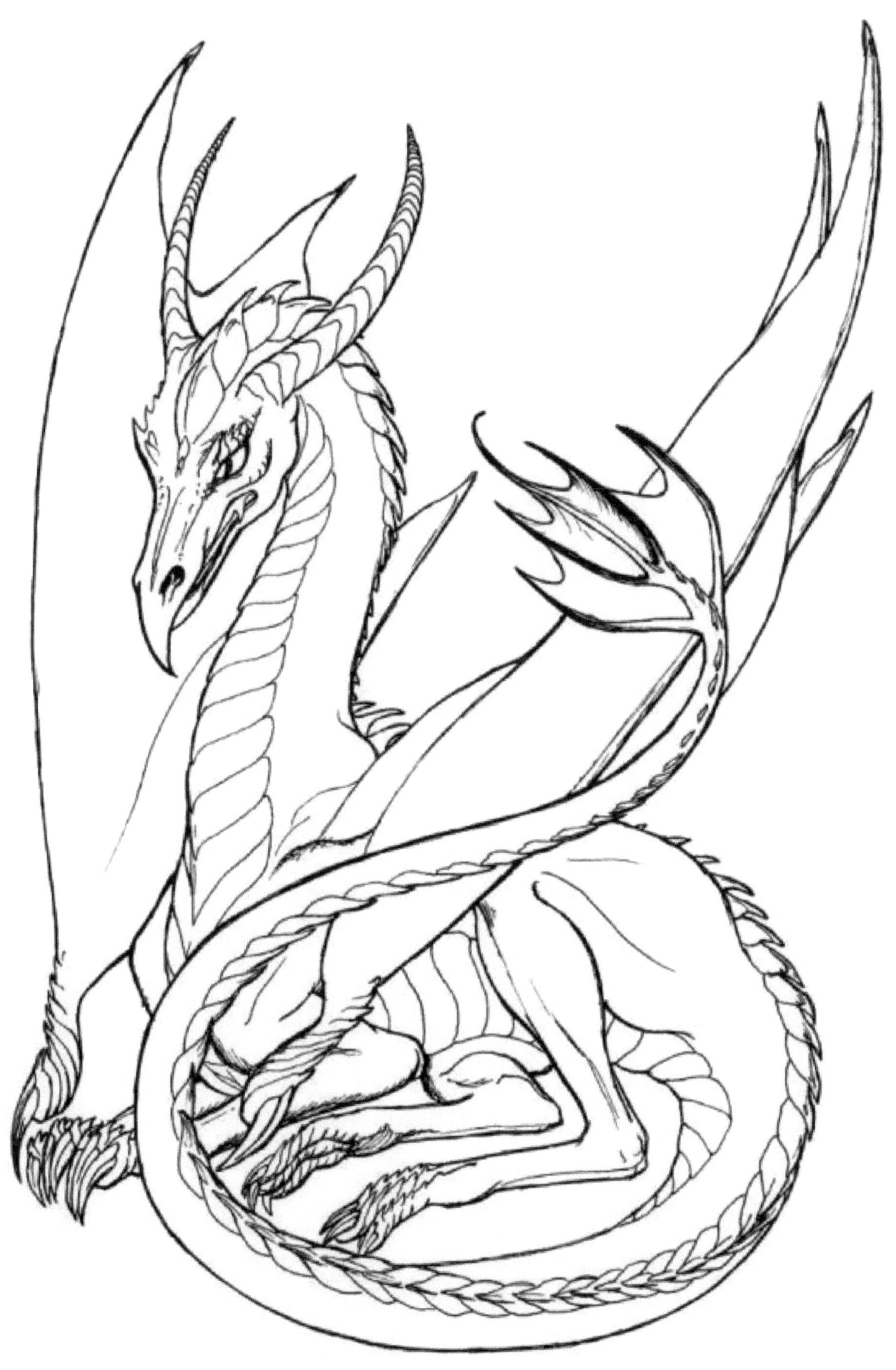

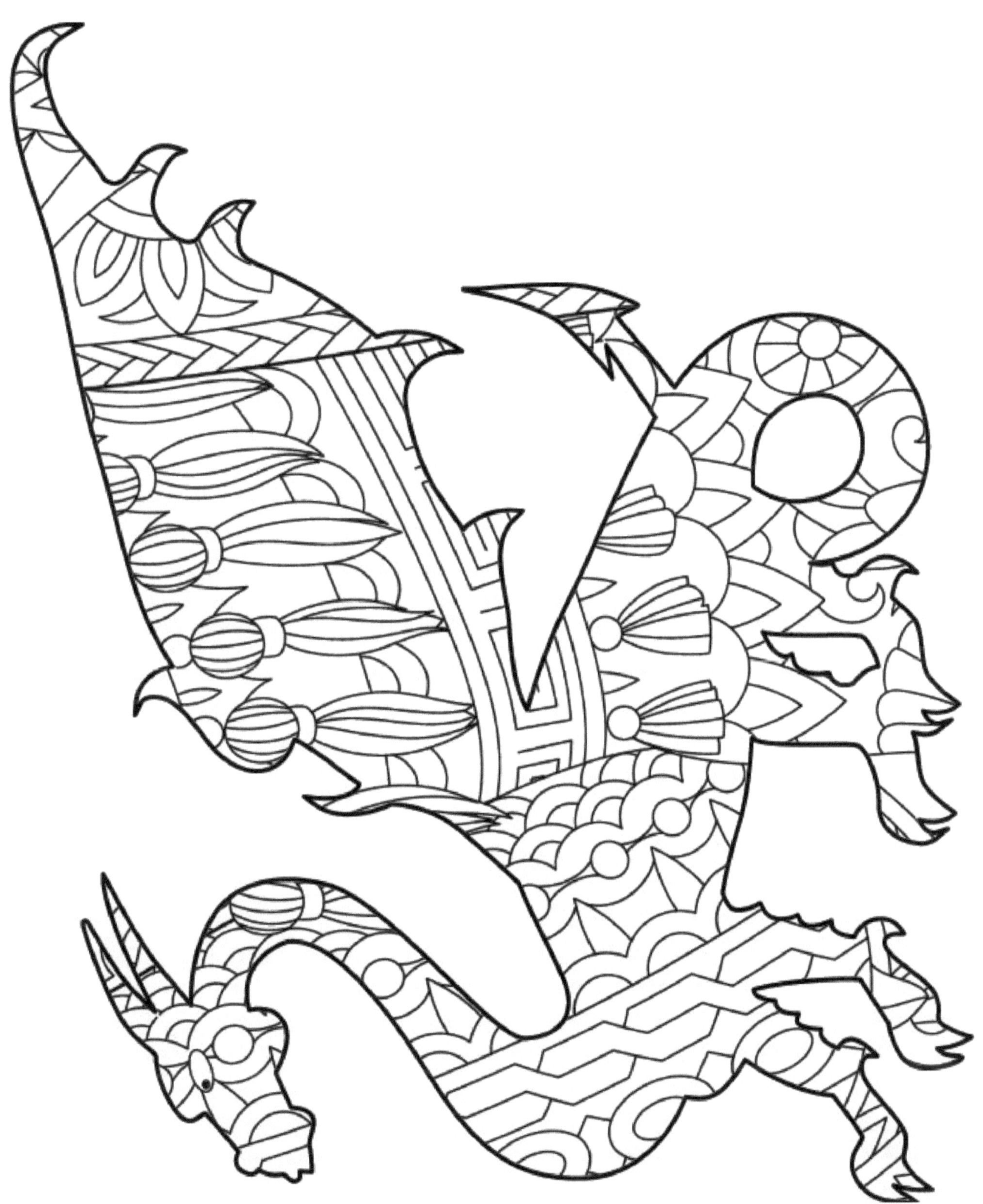

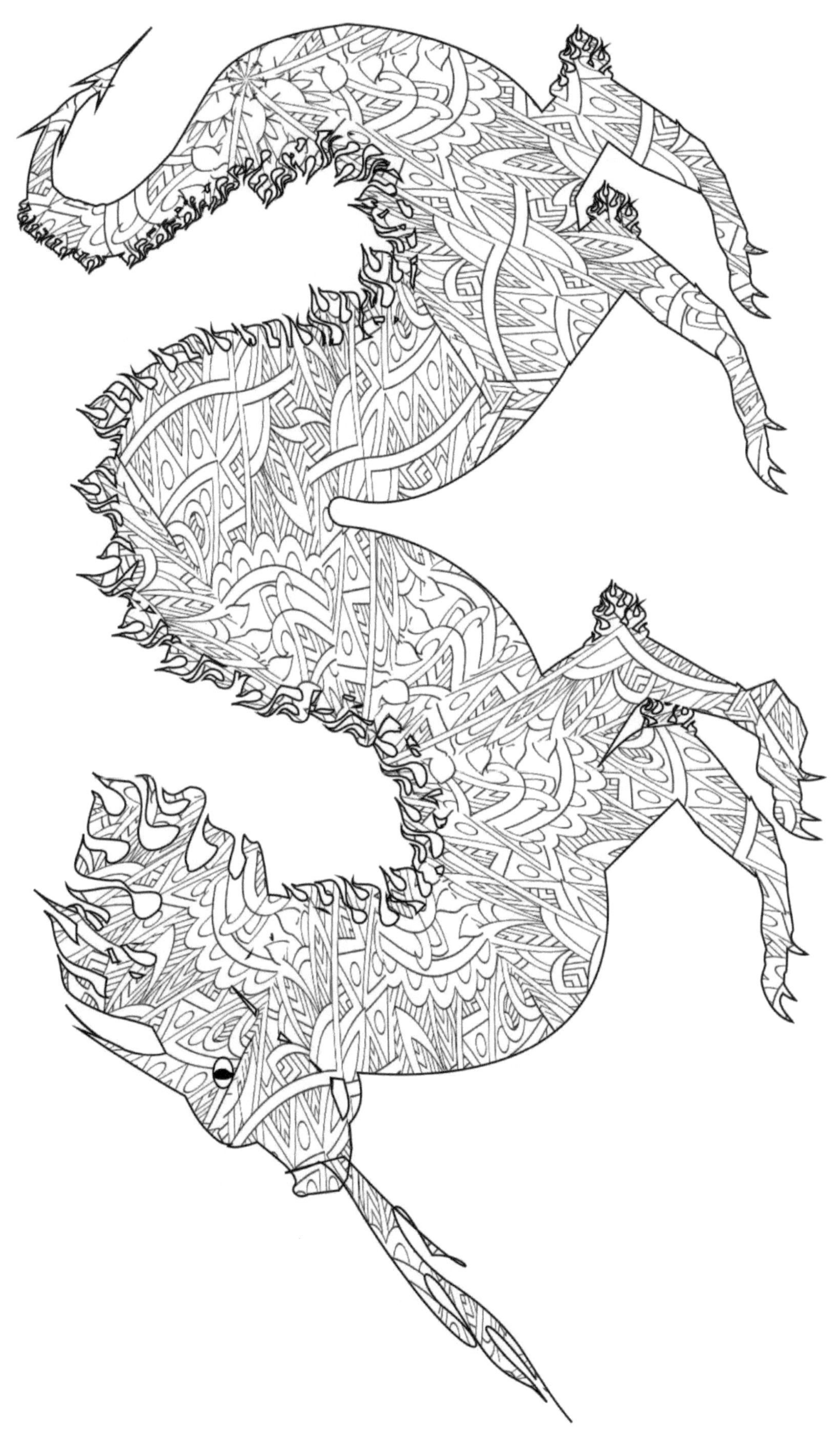

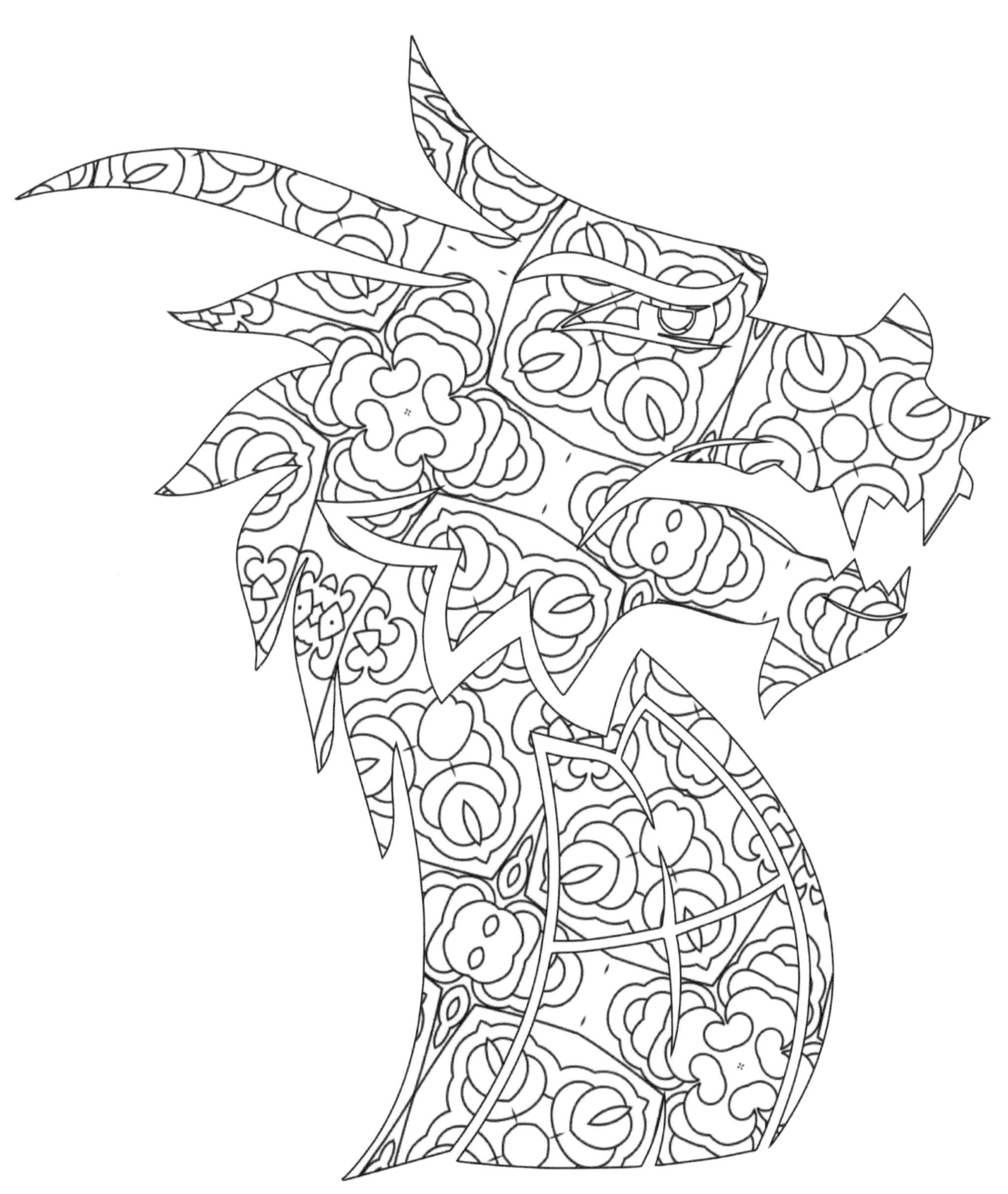

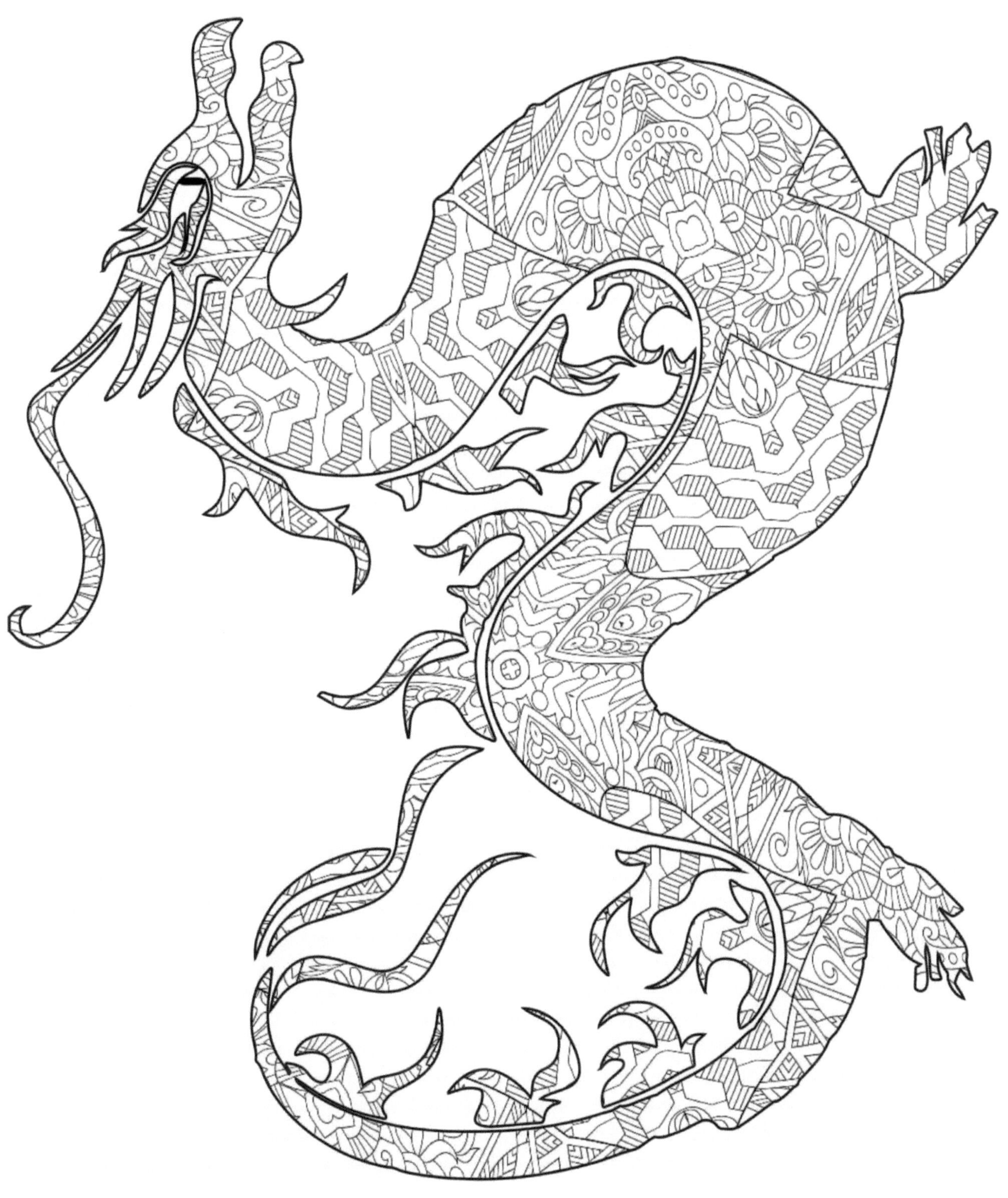

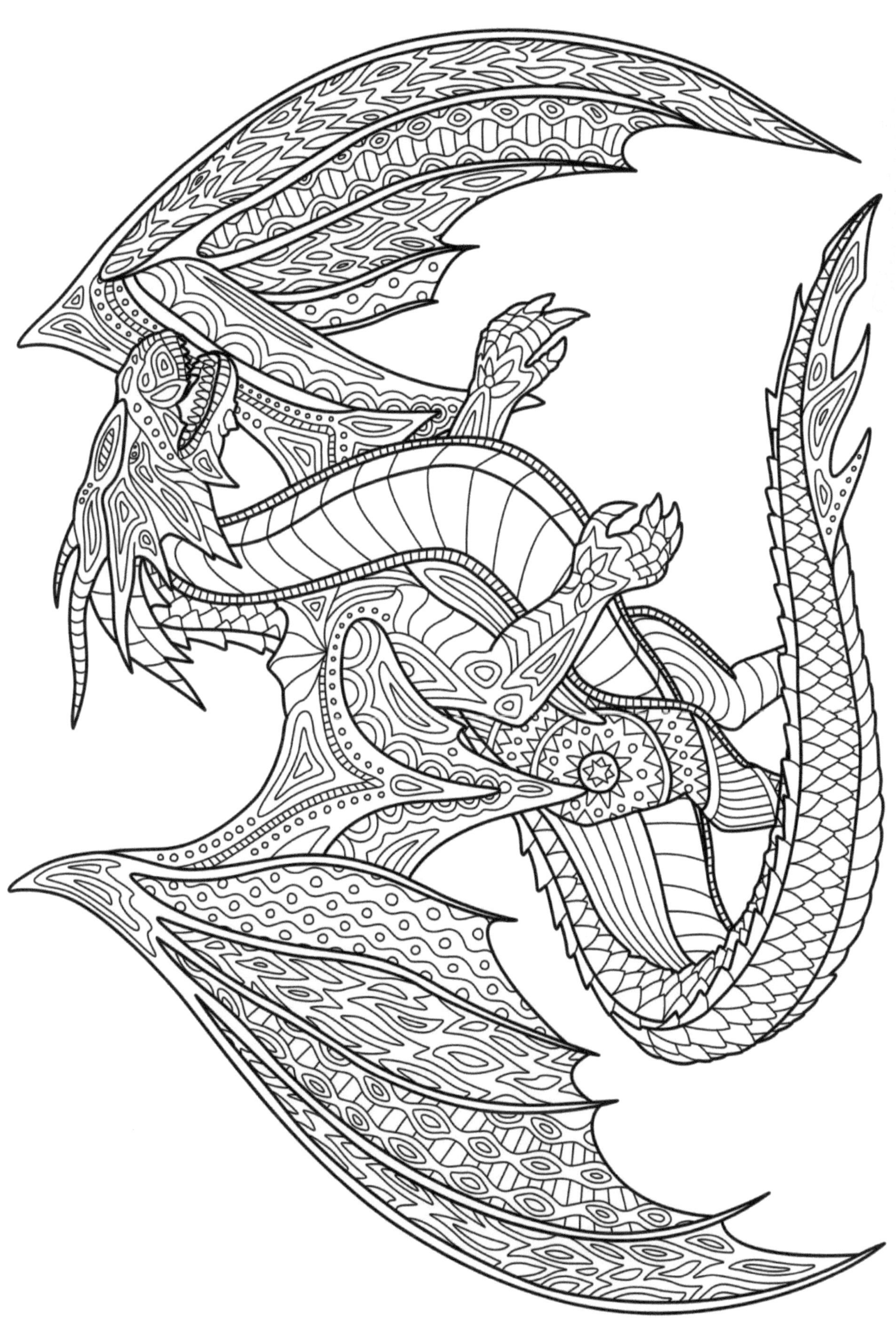

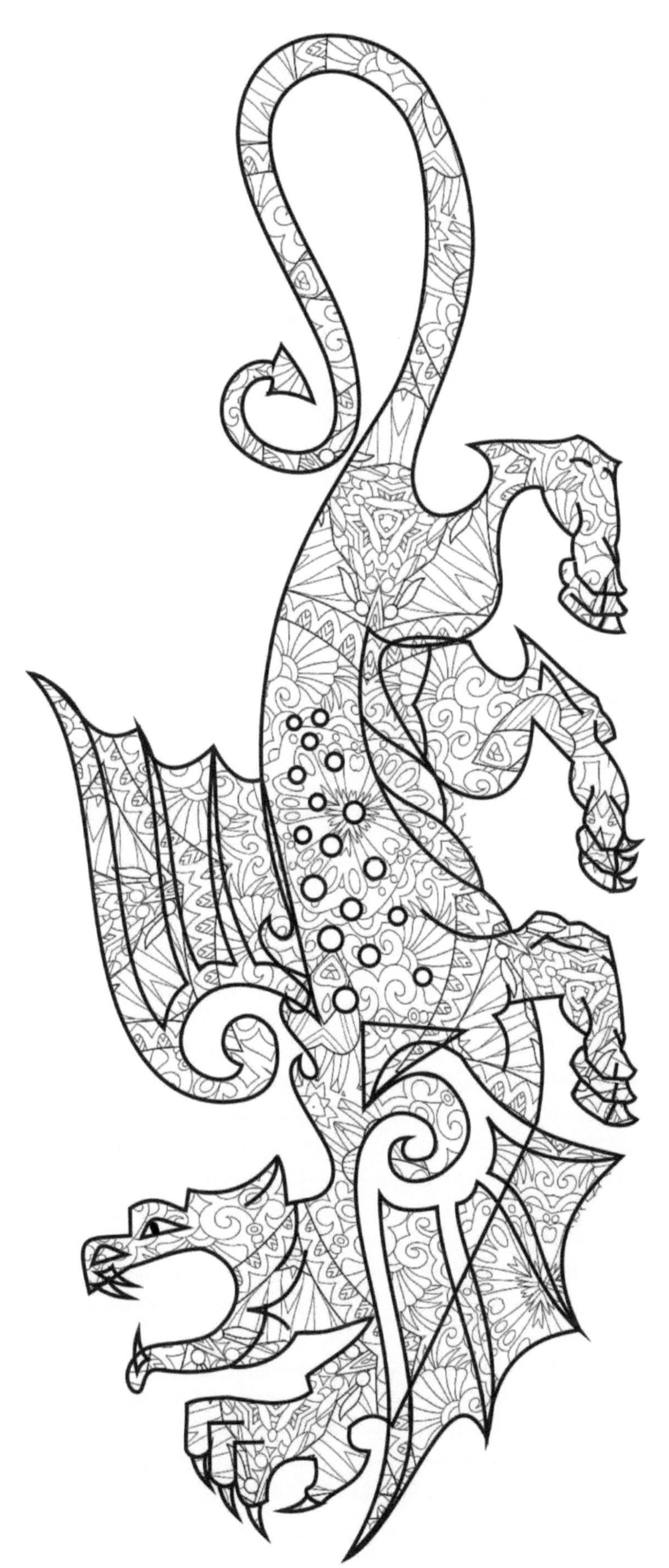

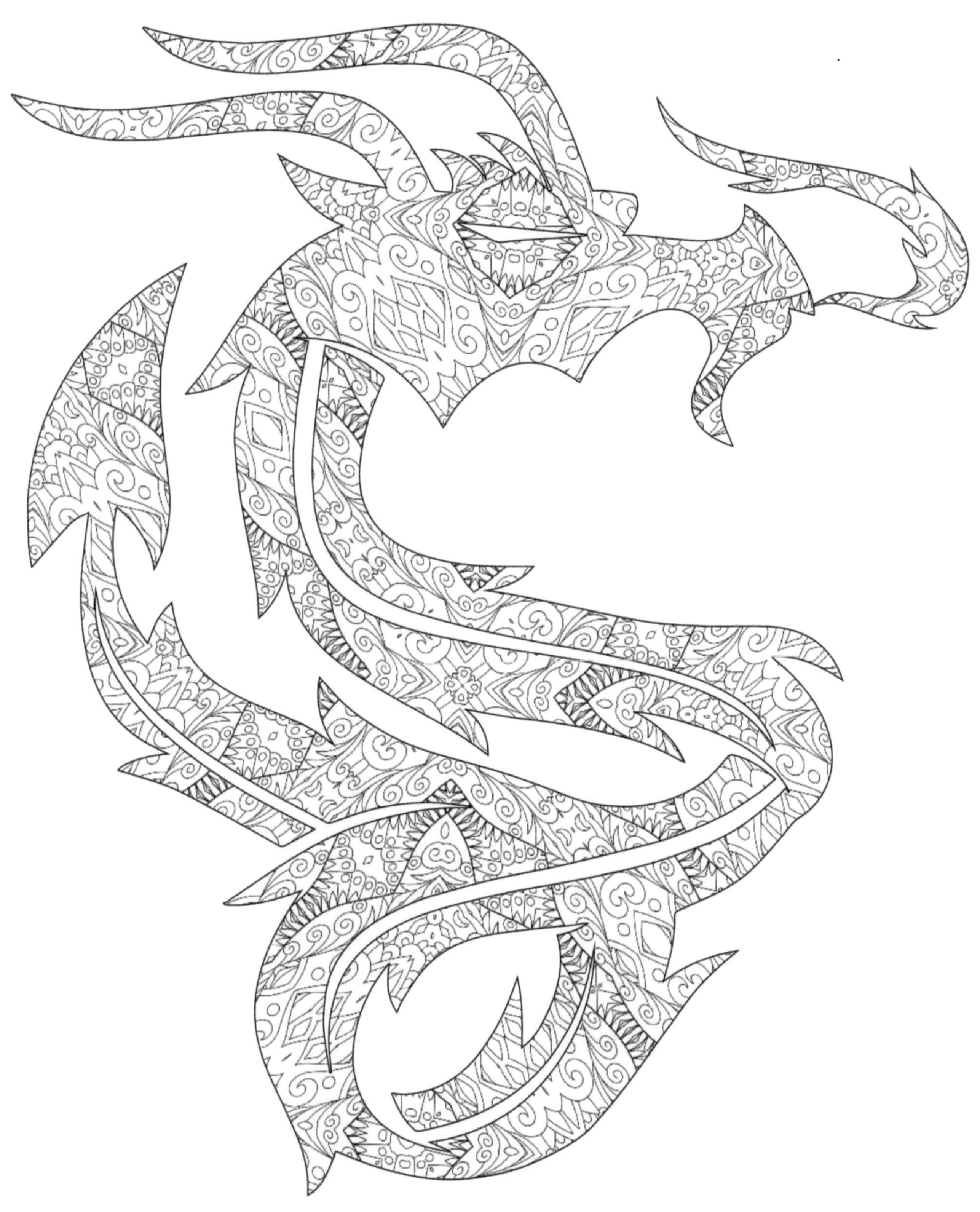

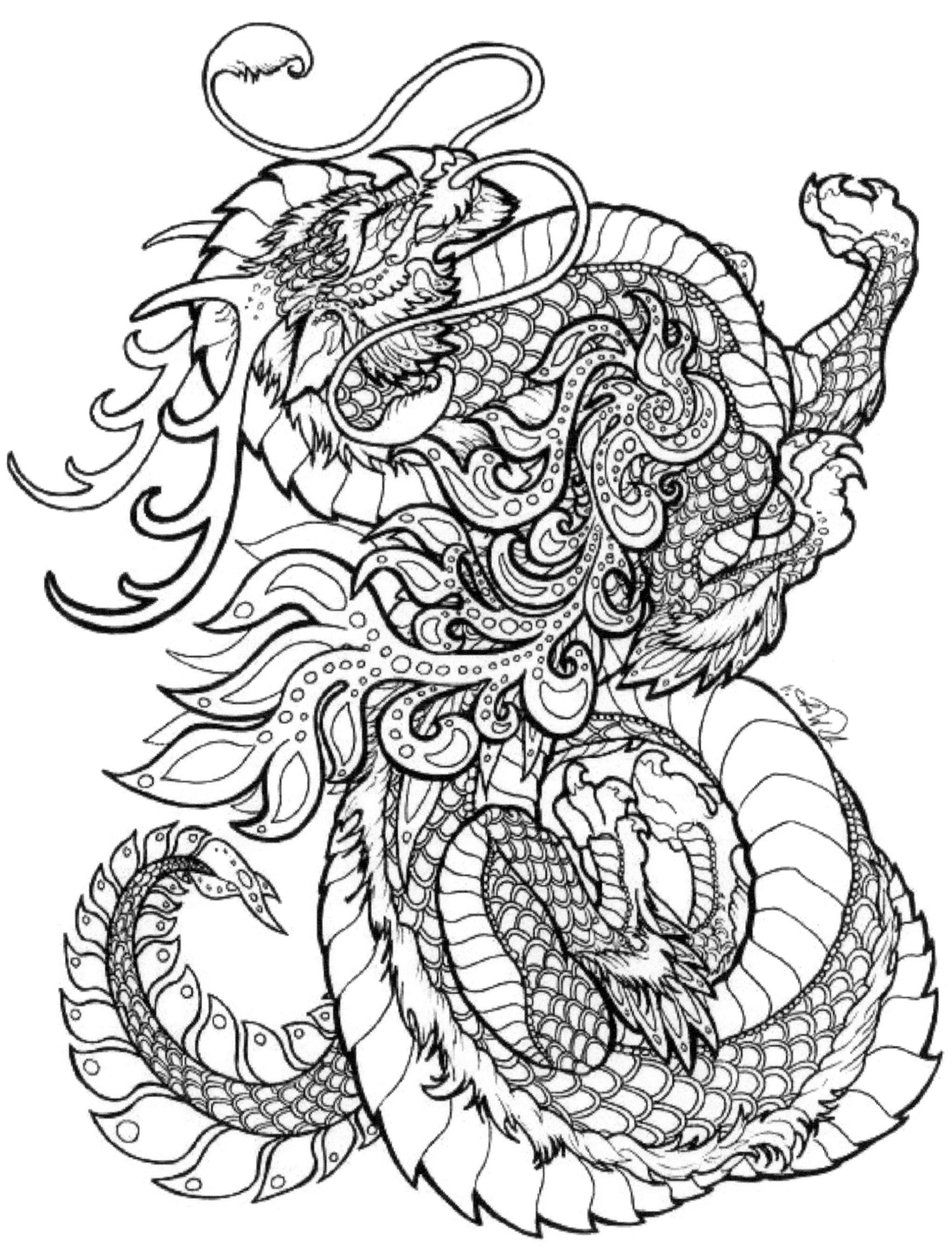

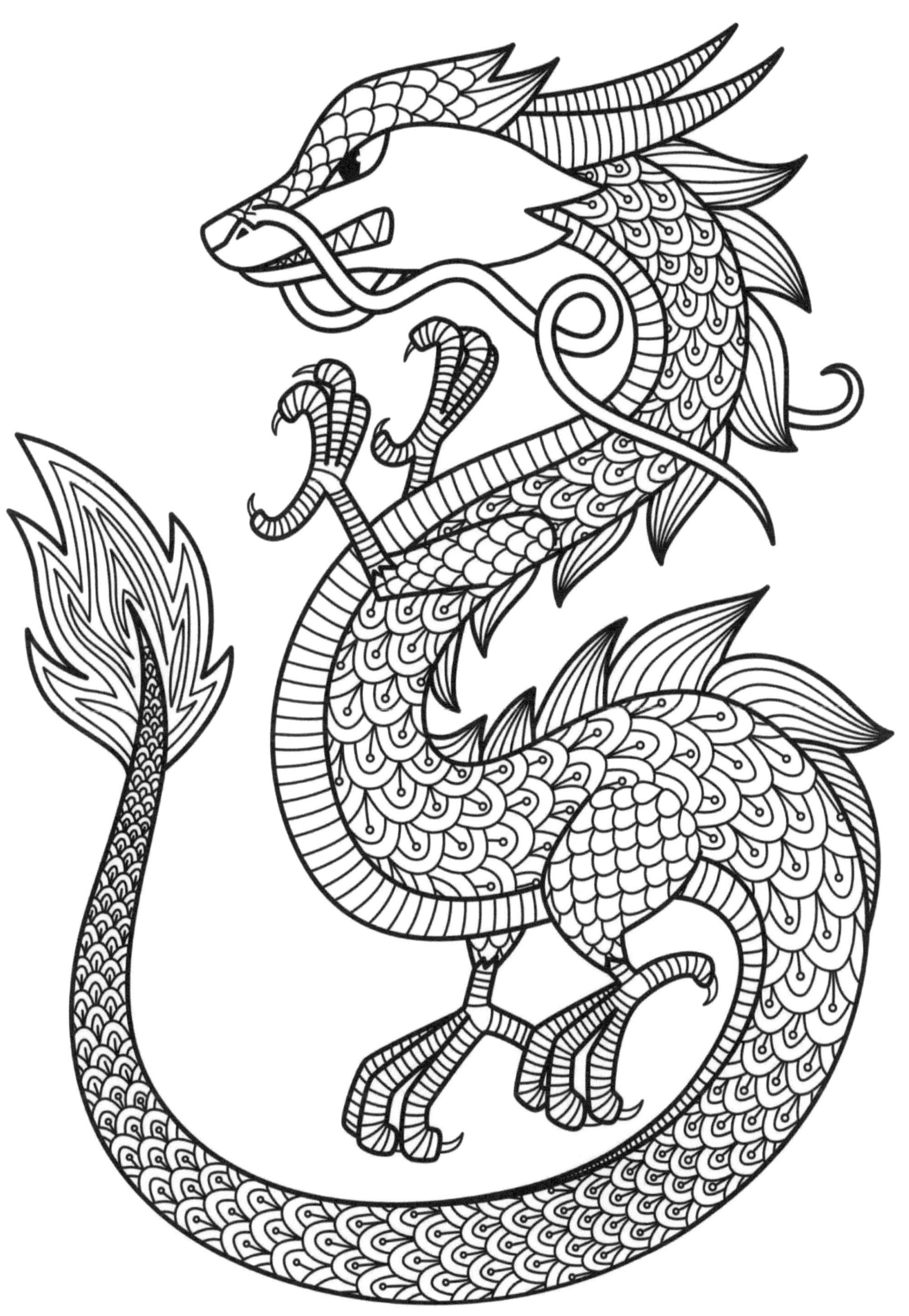

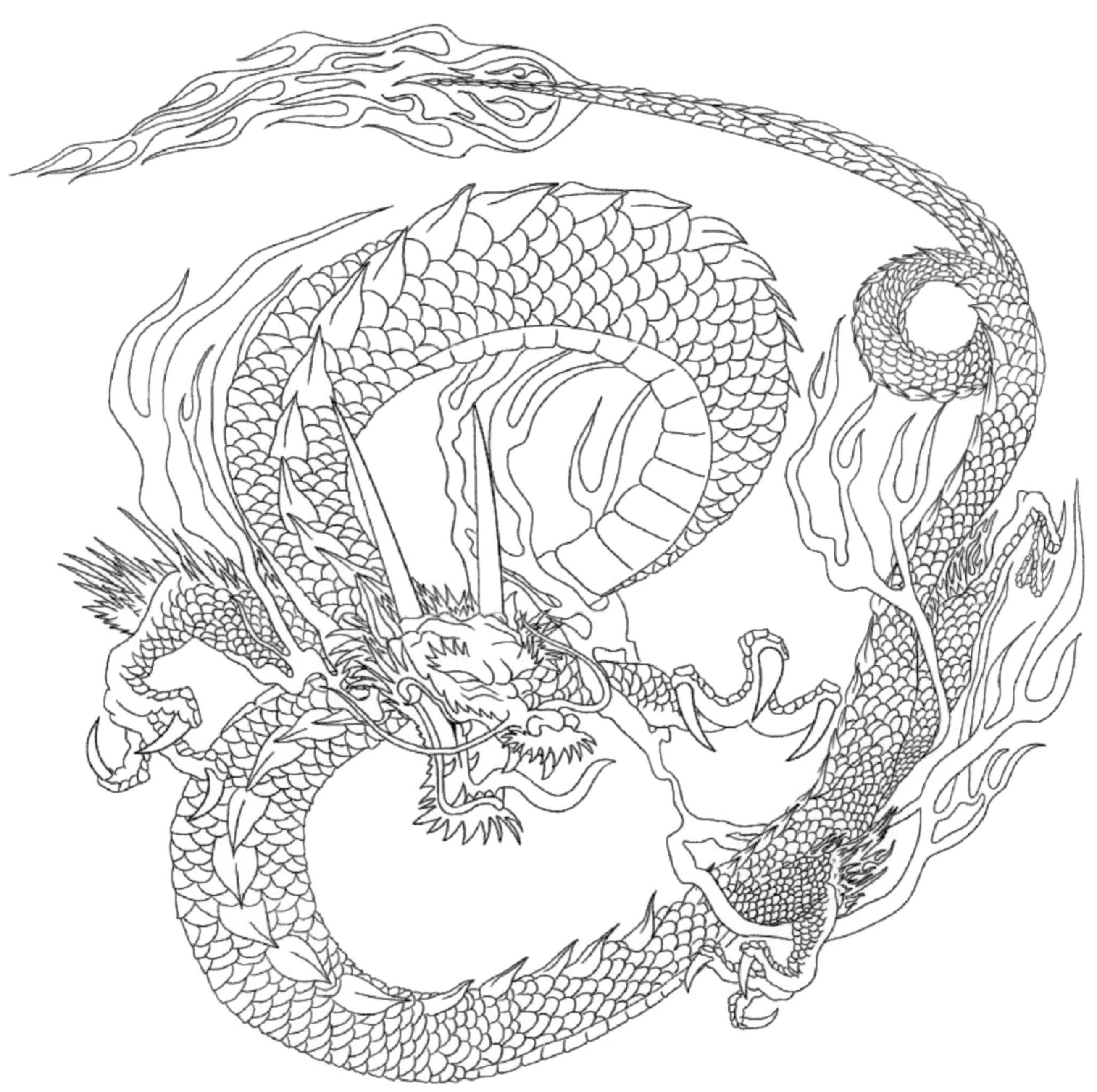

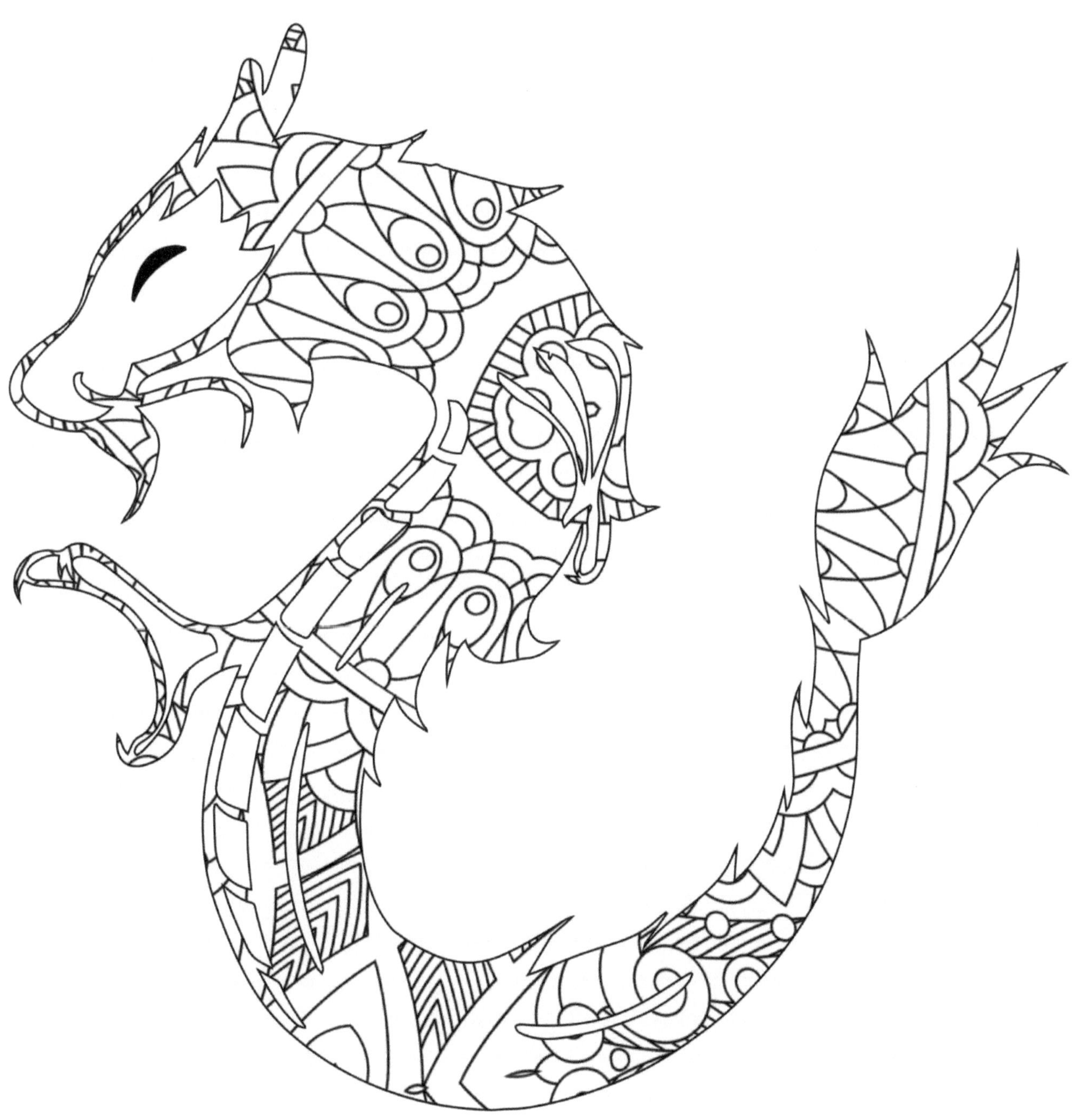

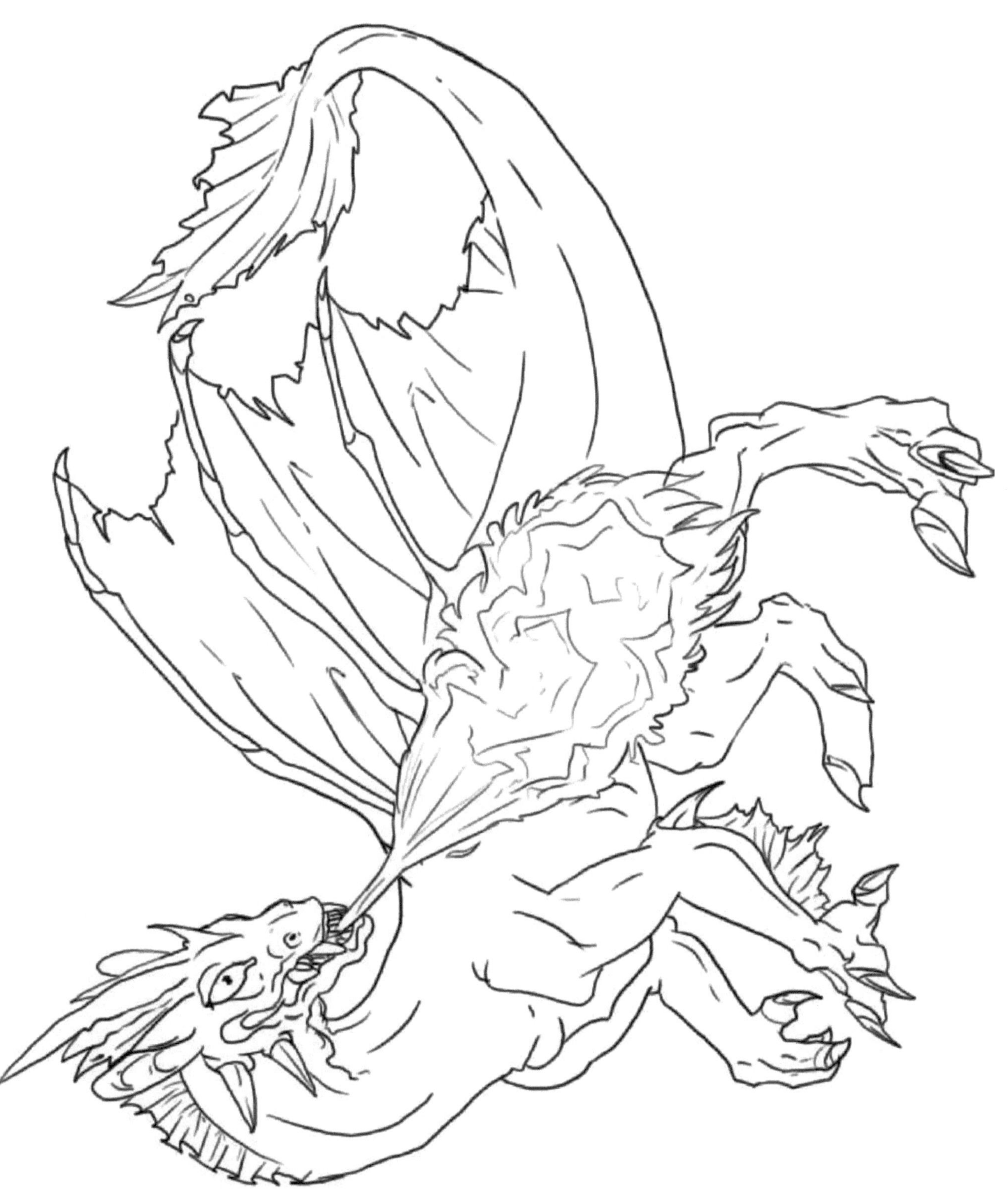

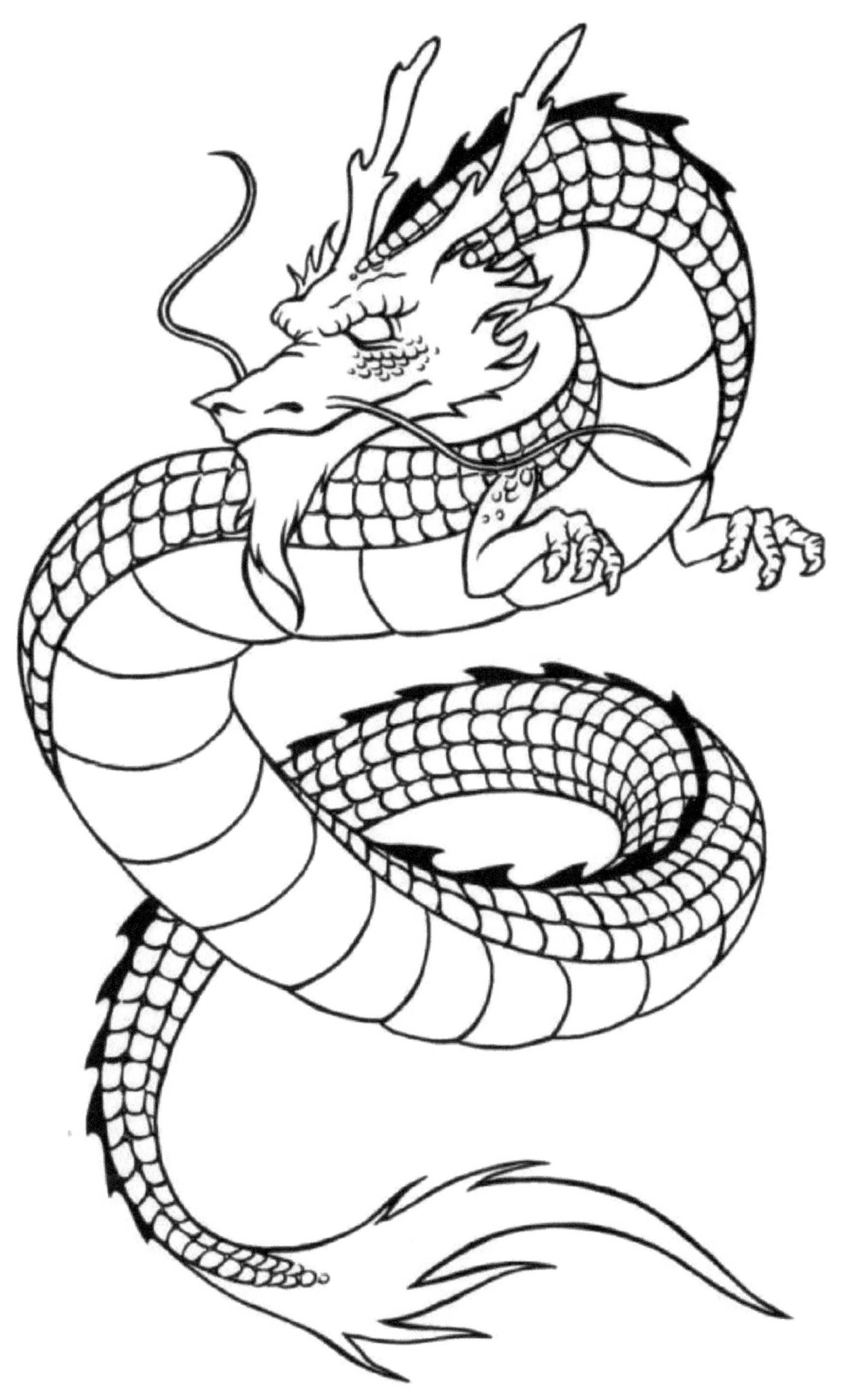

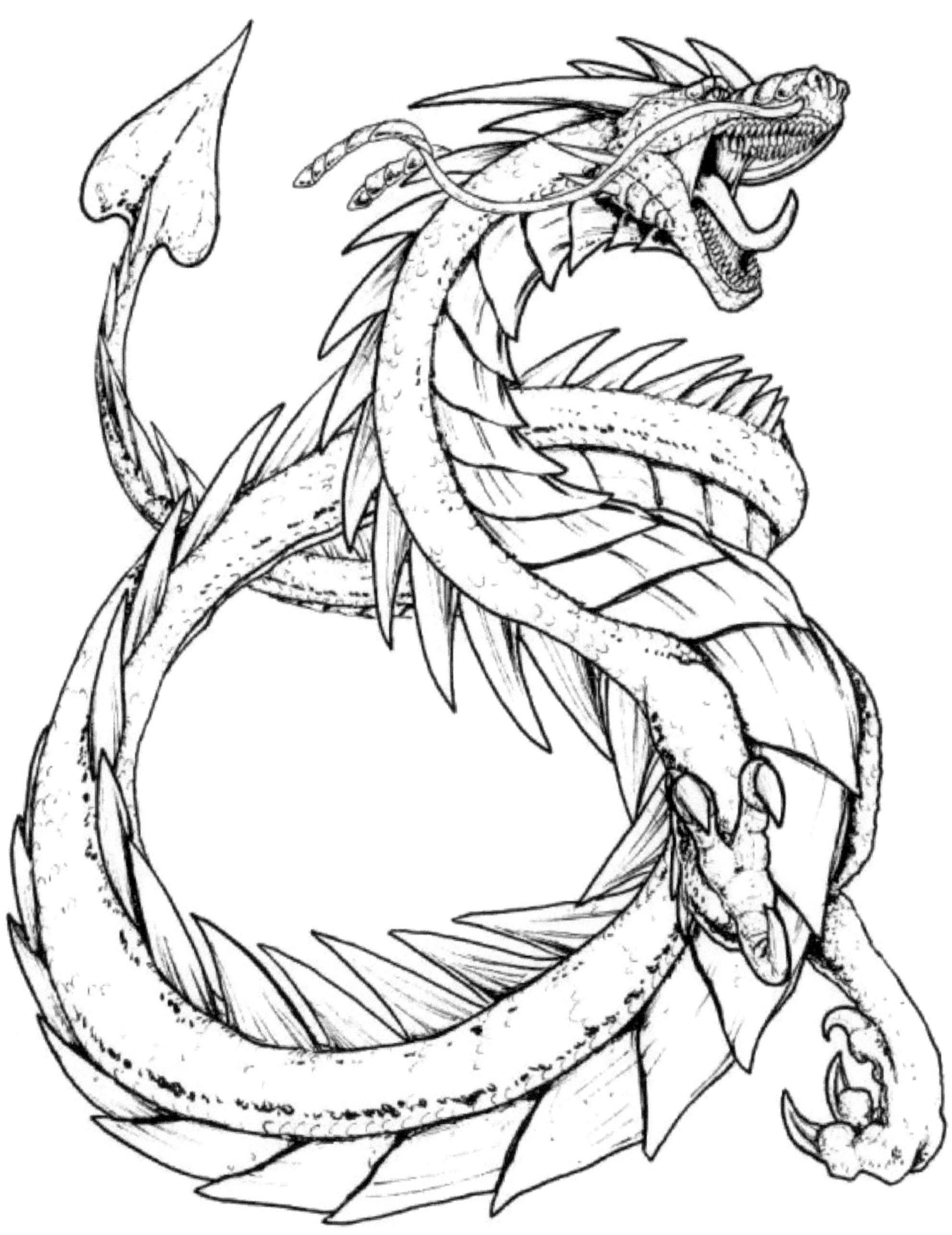

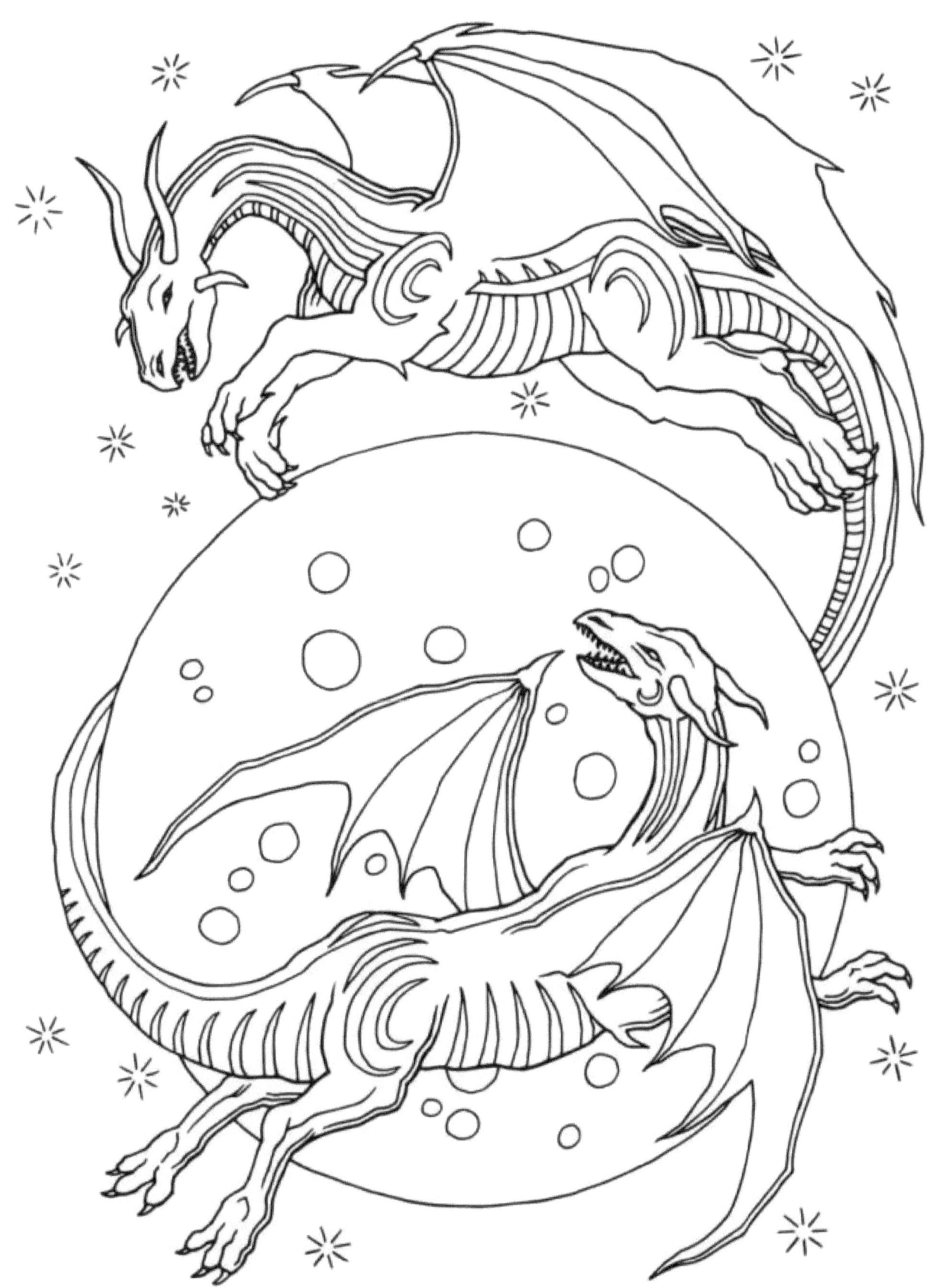

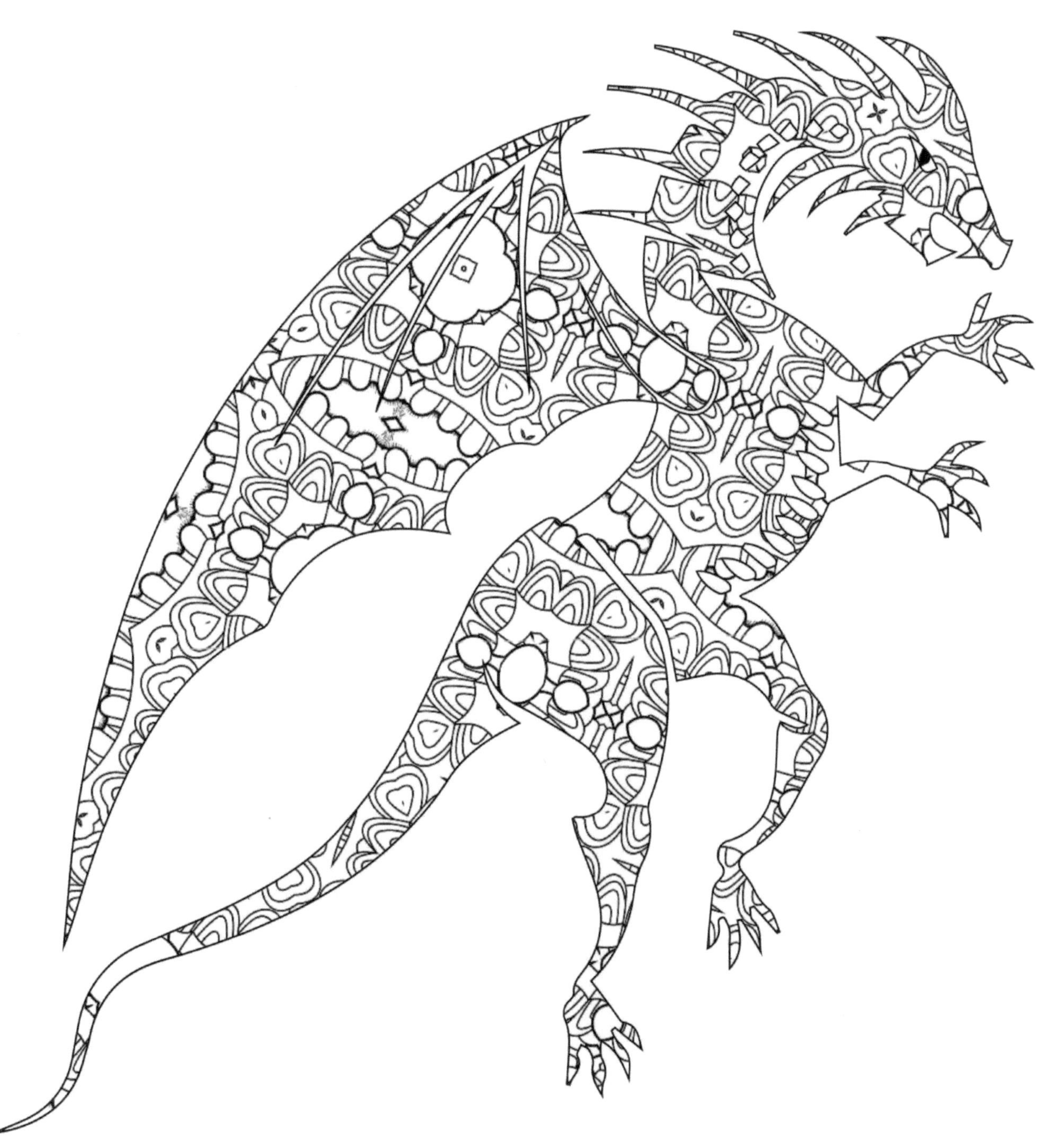

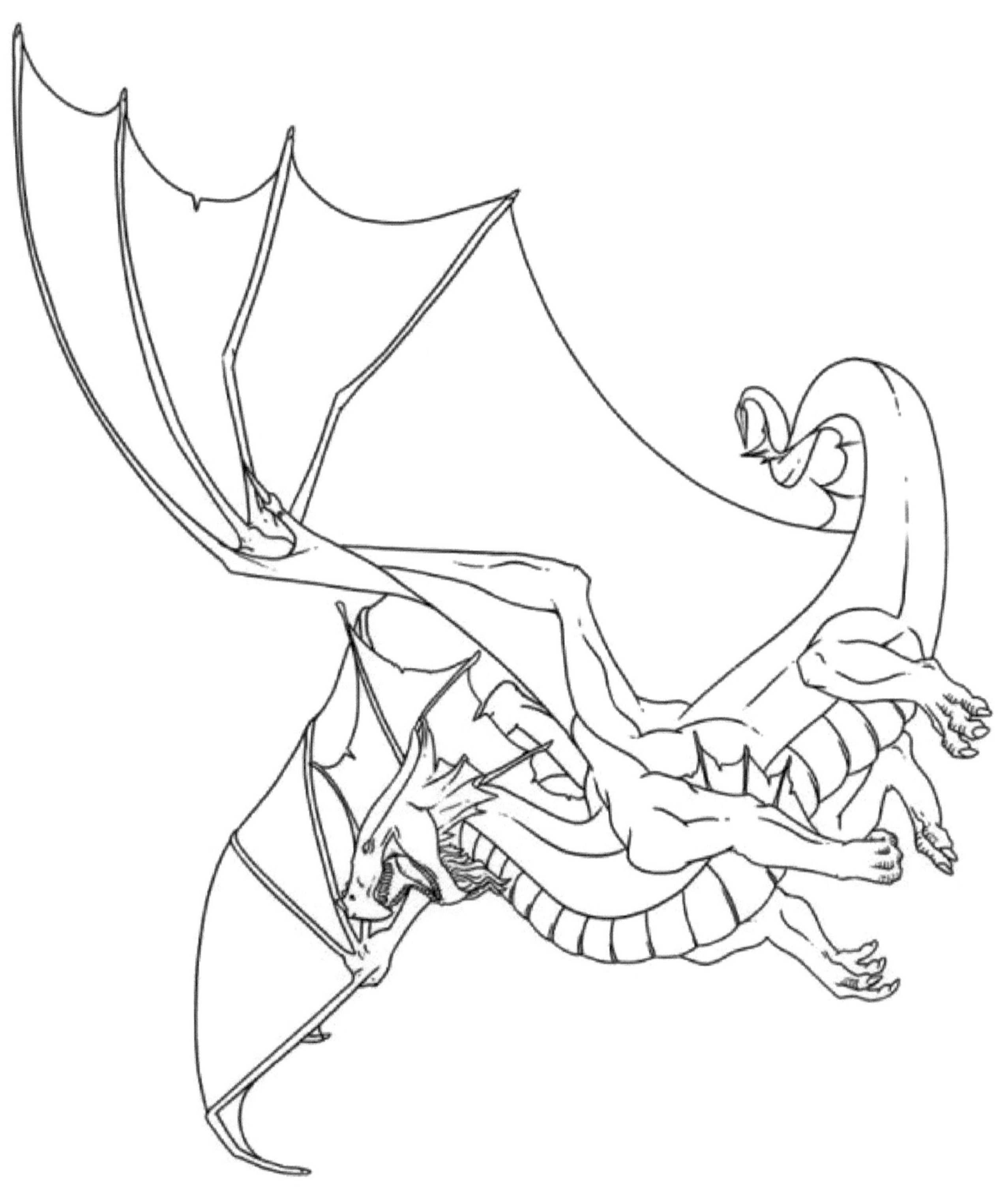

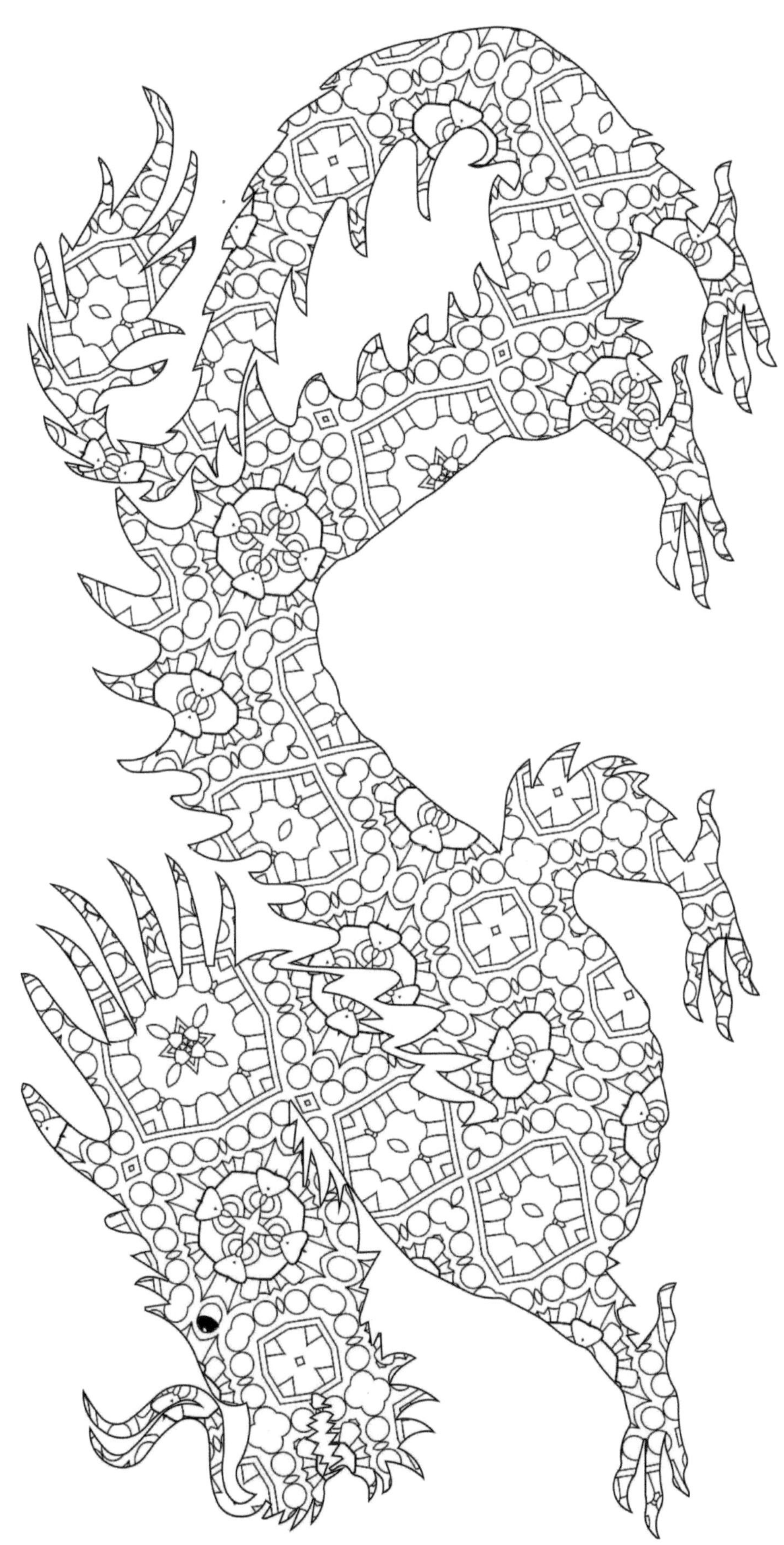

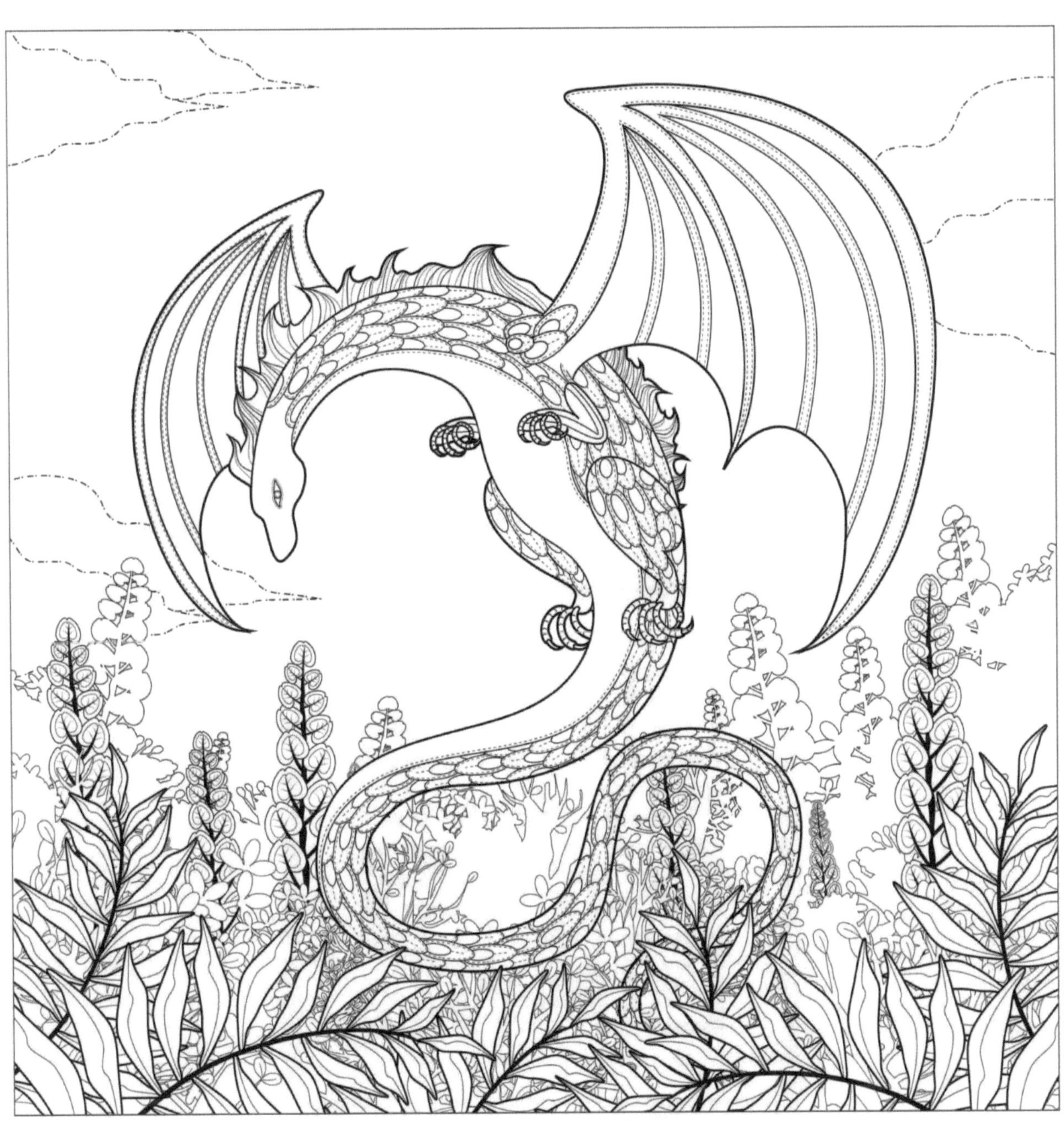

THANK YOU FOR YOUR PURCHASE

Scan the QR Code to Get your Free Coloring Pages

Printed by Libri Plureos GmbH in Hamburg,
Germany